The SECRET of the
HAUNTED MIRROR

Alfred Hitchcock
and The Three Investigators in

The SECRET of the
HAUNTED
MIRROR

Text by M. V. Carey

Based on characters created by Robert Arthur

Illustrated by Jack Hearne

Random House  New York

Library of Congress Cataloging in Publication Data
Carey, M   V
Alfred Hitchcock and the three investigators in The secret of the haunted mirror.
(Alfred Hitchcock mystery series, 21)
SUMMARY: Three young sleuths discover who is haunting a mysterious old
mirror—and why.
[1. Mystery and detective stories] I. Arthur, Robert. II. Hearne, Jack, illus. III. Title.
IV. Title: The secret of the haunted mirror. V. Series.
PZ7.C213Ap   [Fic]   74-5750
ISBN 0-394-82820-8   ISBN 0-394-92820-2 (lib. bdg.)

Manufactured in the United States of America   3   4   5   6   7   8   9   0

Contents

A Word
from Alfred Hitchcock

For those of you who already know The Three Investigators, this introduction is quite unnecessary. You may turn immediately to Chapter One and proceed with the adventure.

If you have not yet encountered Jupiter Jones, Pete Crenshaw, and Bob Andrews, however, I shall be pleased to provide some information about them and their detective firm.

These three remarkable young chaps reside in Rocky Beach, California, a small community near Hollywood. Jupiter Jones, the stout and brainy lad who is First Investigator and leader of the trio, has a mind that is maddeningly efficient and a manner that is, alas, rather pompous. Pete Crenshaw, the Second Investigator, is an athletic but cautious fellow who is often distressed by Jupiter's daring. Bob Andrews, a quiet, bookish boy, is very thorough in his quest for information which may help The Three Investigators solve their cases.

The young detectives make their headquarters in an old mobile home trailer, which sits in a salvage yard owned by Jupiter's uncle. Their activities are not always confined to Rocky Beach. In the case which you will shortly peruse, the boys encounter a ghostly presence in an old mansion in Hollywood—a mansion reputed to be haunted—and they try to find the secret of the man who disappeared into a looking glass and never returned.

Or did he?

Read on and decide for yourself.

ALFRED HITCHCOCK

The SECRET of the HAUNTED MIRROR

1
"Stop, Thief!"

"Uncle Titus is having a wonderful time," said Jupiter Jones. The stocky boy leaned against the fender of a pickup truck belonging to The Jones Salvage Yard. "In one short afternoon he has acquired four stained glass windows, one marble mantelpiece, an antique bathtub, and seven mahogany doors."

Pete Crenshaw groaned and sat down on the curb. "I don't think it was such a short afternoon," he complained. "Not when we had to load all that stuff on the truck. That bathtub weighed a ton!"

Bob Andrews grinned. "It was a lot of work," he said, "but it's fun to watch Jupe's uncle when he's on a buying spree."

Jupe rubbed his forearm across his brow. Right after lunch he, Bob, and Pete had left Rocky Beach with Uncle Titus. An old house in the hills above

Hollywood was to be torn down, and Uncle Titus was determined to salvage what he could from it. Now it was almost four o'clock, and the August sun beat fiercely on the hills. Below, the city seemed to shimmer in waves of heat.

"Jupe," said Pete, "what's your uncle doing in there so long?"

"Doubtless, he is making sure that he has not overlooked any treasures," said Jupiter Jones.

The other boys nodded. The Jones Salvage Yard, which was owned by Jupiter's uncle and aunt, was famed up and down the Pacific Coast for the variety of items it offered for sale. Uncle Titus regularly scouted Los Angeles in search of antique doors, unusual lighting fixtures, gates, fences, hardware, and used furniture. Sometimes he bought things that were extremely difficult to resell. This caused Aunt Mathilda to scold a bit, but she always directed Hans and Konrad, the two Bavarian brothers who helped out at the salvage yard, to make room for the latest curiosity. In the long run, even the strangest pieces of furniture or paneling could be sold, and then Uncle Titus felt triumphant indeed.

Jupiter smiled as Uncle Titus finally emerged from the huge, mock-Victorian mansion which perched at the top of Crestview Drive. Mr. Jones stood for a moment talking to the boss of the wrecking crew which would shortly tear the house down to make way for a new apartment complex. The two men shook hands, and Uncle Titus came down the walk to the truck.

"Okay, boys," he said. "Nothing worthwhile left there. It's a pity, too. They don't build houses like that any more. It must have been magnificent when it was new. Now there are termites everywhere—and dry rot." Uncle Titus sighed, brushed at his big black mustache, and climbed into the cab of the truck. "Let's go!" he cried.

In seconds the boys had stowed themselves in the back of the truck amid the mahogany doors and the stained glass windows. The truck began to roll slowly down the steep grade toward Hollywood. Jupe looked out and saw that most places in the neighborhood were well kept up. The street was lined with very large old houses. Some were built like English country houses, some like French castles, and many were Spanish colonial mansions with stucco walls and heavy, red tile roofs.

"Look!" Bob tapped Jupe's shoulder and pointed to a really enormous Spanish house on the right side of the road. In front of the place there was a car—a very special car. A black Rolls-Royce with gold-plated trim.

"Our special Rolls!" exclaimed Jupiter. "No doubt Worthington is somewhere in the vicinity."

Some time before, Jupiter had won a contest sponsored by the Rent-'n-Ride Auto Company. The prize had been the use of the vintage Rolls for thirty days. With the car had come Worthington, the perfect English chauffeur. He had driven the three boys on many occasions when, as The Three Investigators, they had been involved in solving mysteries, discovering hidden treasures, and thwarting some very evil plans. After the thirty-day prize period had expired, a grateful client had arranged for rental of the Rolls whenever the boys needed transportation.

Uncle Titus slowed the truck and began to edge around the gleaming Rolls. Just then the front door of the big house was snatched open. A small, thin man dressed in a dark suit sped out, running as fast as his skinny legs could carry him.

"Halt! Stop, you scoundrel!"

Worthington raced after the man.

Uncle Titus slammed on the brakes as Pete leaped out of the truck and dashed forward, trying to intercept the fleeing figure.

"Stop, thief!" shouted Worthington.

Pete launched himself at the man, trying to get a grip on his waist. Worthington's quarry was small, but he was agile. His fist shot out and Pete felt a sharp, stunning explosion of pain under his right eye. Then his legs crumpled beneath him, and he fell sideways. Footsteps pounded away and he heard a car door slam.

"Oh, dash it all!" cried Worthington.

Pete opened his eyes and shook his head to clear it. Worthington was bending over him.

"Are you all right, Master Pete?" asked the chauffeur.

"I think so. Just let me catch my breath."

Bob and Jupe came running up to Pete.

"The guy got away," Bob told him. "He had a car parked down the road."

Worthington drew himself up to his full six feet. His long, usually cheerful face was red with anger and exertion. "How could I have let that wretch outrace me?" he exclaimed. Then he began to look slightly cheered. "At least we gave him a good fright!" he announced.

2
The House of Mirrors

"Worthington, did he get away? I've called the police."

Jupiter blinked. Pete rubbed his face in a dazed manner, and Bob gaped at the woman who had appeared in the doorway of the Spanish-style mansion.

"I am afraid he did, madam," said Worthington.

The woman came down the walk. Jupe suddenly realized that his mouth was open, and he shut it. It was not easy to startle Jupiter Jones, but almost anyone would be startled at the sight of a lady dressed in a heavy, wide-skirted brocade gown, complete with hoops. When she was closer Jupe saw that the white hair piled high on her head was really a powdered wig.

"Mrs. Darnley," said Worthington, "I should like

to present my friends, The Three Investigators."

"Oh?" The woman looked puzzled for a moment. Then she smiled. "Oh, yes. The three young detectives. Worthington's told me about you. Now let me see." She nodded toward Jupe. "I think you must be Jupiter Jones."

"Yes," said Jupe.

Worthington then introduced Bob and Pete. "Master Pete attempted to intercept the intruder," he explained.

"You're not hurt, are you?" she asked.

"No, I'm not," said Pete as he stood up slowly.

"Thank goodness. People who break into houses can be quite dangerous, I understand."

Uncle Titus got out of the truck then.

"Mrs. Darnley, this is Mr. Titus Jones," said Worthington.

She smiled broadly. "My, this is a pleasure! I've heard of you and your famous salvage yard. I've been intending to visit you to see if you have any interesting mirrors."

"Mirrors?" said Uncle Titus.

"Yes. I collect them. Do come in and see."

She turned and swept up the walk and into the house, her wide skirt rustling as she walked.

"Does she always dress like that?" asked Pete.

"She is a most interesting lady," said Worthington. "I drive for her rather frequently, as she does not care to keep her own automobile. You'll find her house fascinating."

The house *was* fascinating. The boys and Uncle Titus followed Worthington through an entrance hall that was dim and strangely chilly. To the left, a large staircase climbed majestically to the second floor; beyond it a long, narrow hallway went off to the side, stretching almost the length of the house. To the right, ornate double doors gave onto a room that was too dark to see into. The visitors were led straight ahead into a vast living room—a room where the walls seemed alive with shadows that shifted and pulsed. Heavy drapes shut out the sunlight, and it took the boys a moment to realize that the moving shadows were their own images. They saw themselves reflected in mirrors—dozens of mirrors, perhaps hundreds. They saw reflections of their reflections. The room seemed to be occupied not by three investigators, but by thirty or three hundred.

"Lovely, aren't they?" Mrs. Darnley's image shifted through the mirrors as she appeared at Jupe's elbow.

"I feel kind of dizzy," said Pete.

"Then sit down," advised Mrs. Darnley. She herself perched on a small chair near the fireplace. "My mirrors are almost all old," she told them, "and they all have a story. It's taken me a lifetime to collect them. I started when I was a little girl. Do you remember the story about Alice going through the looking glass and finding that wonderful world where everything was turned around? When I was very young I thought that I could do that if I could only find the right looking glass."

A boy about Pete's age and size came into the room. He had carrot-colored hair and his nose was spattered with freckles. Behind him was a girl who was almost as tall as he, but whose hair was darker. She smiled at Worthington, who stood stiffly near one of the windows. Her eyes went to Uncle Titus and then to the boys.

"These are my grandchildren," said Mrs. Darnley. "Jean and Jeff Parkinson. Children, this is Mr. Titus Jones, who owns the famous salvage yard, his nephew Jupiter, and their friends, Bob and Pete."

"The Three Investigators!" exclaimed Jeff.

"What timing!" said the girl. "Just when we've had a burglar—not that he took anything."

"Nothing is missing?" asked Mrs. Darnley.

"Not so far as we can tell," Jean answered.

They heard a siren then, coming up the hill.

"That'll be the police," said Mrs. Darnley. "Jean, you let them in. And Worthington, please sit down. You look so uncomfortable standing there like a post."

"Yes, madam," said Worthington, and he found a chair.

Jean ushered two young patrolmen into the room. One of them dropped his cap when he saw Mrs. Darnley in her brocade finery. She ignored his surprise and briefly told the policemen what had happened.

"I was upstairs having a cup of tea," she said. "My houseman, John Chan, was with me. He was serving.

Neither of us heard anything unusual. Doubtless the burglar thought there was no one in the house. However, when Worthington and my grandchildren came back from Farmers' Market, they surprised the housebreaker. He was in the library, and so far as we know he took nothing. Perhaps he didn't have time."

Worthington and the boys then described the person who had fled from the house—short, very thin, dark-haired and wiry, middle-aged but strong and quick. Jupiter described the car in which the man had made his escape.

"Thousands of cars like that," said one of the policemen. "Did you get the license number?"

"I'm sorry, I didn't," said Jupiter. "There was mud on the car and on the plate."

The policeman wrote something in his notebook and sighed.

"We know how he got in," said Jean Parkinson. "He broke the lock on the kitchen door."

The policeman nodded. "Old story," he said. "Back doors never have good locks."

"My back door has . . . that is, it did have a very good lock," said Mrs. Darnley. "I am careful about these things. You may have noticed that all the windows in this house are covered with iron grillwork. There are only two doors, the front one and the one from the kitchen out to the garage. They both have double dead-bolt locks. The man forced the door with a crowbar. Jeff, take the officers to the kitchen and show them!"

The men retreated, led by Jeff, and very shortly they returned. One of them was carrying the crowbar which the burglar had used to get into the house.

"The fingerprint men may be able to do something with this," he said.

"The man was wearing gloves," said Pete.

"You sure?"

"I'm certain. I ought to know. He took a swipe at me."

The policemen left then, promising to contact Mrs. Darnley if they had any leads which might enable them to identify the burglar. Worthington left, too, to return the Rolls to the auto rental company.

"That's probably the last we'll hear about that," said Mrs. Darnley. "Well, no great harm done. Would you like to see the house? It used to belong to Drakestar, the magician. He built it."

"Drakestar's house?" Jupiter, who knew a great deal about theatrical people, suddenly sat straighter. "So this is Drakestar's house? I've read about it."

Mrs. Darnley nodded. "Drakestar died here, and the place is supposed to be haunted. I've never seen or heard anything odd, myself. But come along, if you like old, interesting things."

She crossed the living room and opened a pair of double doors. Uncle Titus, The Three Investigators, and Jean and Jeff Parkinson followed her into a huge dining room. Here the drapes were open, and the western sun shone in and touched walls which were covered with a heavy red damask. Over the sideboard was a looking glass framed with gilt scrolls. It appeared to be very old, and in several places the silver backing had pulled away from the glass.

"That's one of my special treasures," said Mrs. Darnley. "It came from the palace of the czars in St. Petersburg. One can't be sure, of course, but perhaps Catherine the Great saw herself in it. That's the fascinating thing about mirrors. They've held so many images, and it's easy to imagine that a little bit of each person stays in the mirror."

Beyond the dining room there was a butler's pantry and beyond that the kitchen, where the boys met John Chan, Mrs. Darnley's houseman. He was slender, somewhere in his mid-twenties, and although it was plain that his ancestors had come from the Orient, he spoke English with a Boston accent. He reported that a carpenter and a locksmith had been called and that the kitchen door would be fixed before dark.

"Good," said Mrs. Darnley. She waved toward a doorway. "John's room is there," she said, "and he won't let me put any mirrors in it."

The houseman smiled. "I see myself coming and going too much as it is," he explained.

"So we'll go on to some of my other treasures." She opened another door and stepped into the long, narrow corridor that the visitors had seen when they first entered the house.

"In Drakestar's day," she said, "this front half of the house was a ballroom. I've had interior walls put in and made a series of . . . well, I suppose you could call the rooms historical displays."

They crowded into a corner room which had walls painted the color of adobe clay. There was a narrow bed, a leather-covered trunk, one wooden chair, and a table made of hand-hewn boards. Over the table was a simple mirror in a maple frame.

"That mirror was brought to California during the gold rush," she said. "It was ordered from New England by an American man who wanted to marry the daughter of a Spanish don. It was a courting present for the girl."

"Did she marry him?" asked Bob.

"Yes, she did, and that was a tragedy. He turned out to be a gambler and he lost everything. This is a reproduction of the room she lived in. At the end of her life she had nothing—absolutely nothing."

The next room was a prim and proper parlor, and Mrs. Darnley called it her Victoria room.

"It's a reproduction of the parlor where Queen Victoria used to sit with her mother when she was a very young girl, before she was queen. The furniture was made to order, but the mirror over the mantel is one she actually owned. Or her mother owned it. I like to think of Victoria looking into that glass, being so young and innocent, and with all those years of greatness ahead of her. I sit here sometimes, and I have a special dress to wear when I do. I don't pretend I'm young Victoria. I'm much too old. Sometimes I pretend I'm her mother."

She then showed them what she called the Lincoln room. It was a dark, shuttered, cluttered chamber. "This is a replica of the room which was used by Mary Todd Lincoln when she was a tired, lonely old woman, long after President Lincoln died. That mirror belonged to her."

Next to Jupiter, Uncle Titus shifted restlessly. "A sad room," he said.

"Very sad," agreed Mrs. Darnley, "but then, many famous people are famous because of some great sorrow."

She closed the door on the little room and became suddenly brisk. "My Marie Antoinette room is upstairs. I have a little hand mirror that belonged to the queen and a few other trinkets that she used. This dress I have on was copied from one of her portraits."

"I see," said Jupiter softly. "Is that a sad room, too?"

"Perhaps it is, in a way," said Mrs. Darnley. "It's a pretty room. I like to sit in it, and I try not to think of how she died—poor, silly little queen. I'll show you the room. It's a copy of one at the palace of Versailles. But first, you'll have to see the latest addition to my collection."

"It's a real horror," said Jean Parkinson.

"We can guarantee you'll hate it," added Jeff.

"It *is* ugly," admitted Mrs. Darnley, "but I'm very proud of it. She rustled the rest of the way down the corridor and crossed the entrance hall. Uncle Titus and the boys followed her past double doors into the dark room they had glimpsed earlier. As soon as Mrs. Darnley opened the drapes, they knew they were in the library. Three walls were lined solidly with books. The fourth wall, the one nearest the street, was paneled with dark wood. There were two long windows, and between these was a mirror that reached almost from the floor to the ceiling.

"Yikes!" exclaimed Pete.

The mirror itself was not unusual. It reflected the boys and Uncle Titus clearly and without any distortion. But the frame was grotesque. A metallic substance had been molded into a series of strangely repellent shapes. There were tangles of tree roots which parted here and there to reveal little faces—the faces of creatures which were not quite human. Some of the sculpted beings had horns on their foreheads. Some had tiny slits for eyes. Some seemed to chuckle with evil glee. At the very top of the frame a stunted, twisted figure with pointed ears was fondling a snake.

"Wha . . ." Bob pointed. "What are those things supposed to be?"

"In Spain the word would be *trasgos*," said Mrs. Darnley. "We'd call them goblins. That mirror belonged to a magician, a man named Chiavo who lived in Madrid almost two hundred years ago. He claimed that he could look into the mirror and see the earth spirits, the goblins, and that they predicted the future for him."

"They were supposed to live in caves and underneath trees and in damp, creepy places like that," said

Jeff. "And they were friends with snakes and worms."

"Ugh!" said Jean Parkinson.

"I am very proud of this glass," said Mrs. Darnley again. "All of my mirrors have stories and many have seen great beauty and great tragedy, but the Chiavo glass is supposed to be truly an enchanted mirror, if one can believe that sort of thing."

She looked, thought Jupiter Jones, like a woman who hoped that a mirror really could be enchanted.

Behind them, in the entrance hall, the doorbell chimed.

"That's probably Señor Santora," said Jean. She grinned at The Three Investigators. "Señor Santora's a man from Spain. He's a collector like Grandma—a real mirror nut—and he wants to buy that mirror with all its nasty little goblins. Comes every day, just about this time."

The doorbell rang again.

Mrs. Darnley looked from the mirror to the entrance hall and then back at the mirror. "Every day," she said. "He has come every day for more than a week, and today . . ."

She stopped, leaving the thought unspoken.

"Today," said Jupiter Jones quietly, "a housebreaker was discovered in this very room."

"But no one could swipe that mirror," protested Jeff. "The frame's steel and it weighs a ton. It took three men to get it up on the wall."

Mrs. Darnley lifted her chin and her face took on a stern expression. "Mr. Jones," she said to Uncle

Titus, "I'd appreciate it if you and the boys would stay and see Señor Santora. Worthington seems to have great respect for The Three Investigators. I'd value their opinion of the man."

Again the doorbell rang.

Mrs. Darnley didn't wait for Uncle Titus to answer. "Let Señor Santora in," she said to Jean.

3

The Curse of Chiavo

The man Jean ushered into the library was rather
heavyset, with very dark hair and wide dark eyes. He
wore a light-colored suit of some expensive material
which had a silky sheen to it. His face was smooth,
unmarked by time or care, but it was a bit flushed, as
if by anger.

"Señora Darnley, if you please . . ." he began.
Then he saw Uncle Titus and The Three Investigators
and he stopped and scowled. His lips tightened. "I
had hoped to find that you were . . . were . . ." He
paused, as if in his mind he was translating a phrase
from Spanish. "I had hoped to find that you were not
with guests," he said finally.

"Won't you all please sit down," said Mrs. Darnley, seating herself. She nodded coolly to Señor Santora. "I have been telling my friends here about the

pride of my collection—the goblin glass."

"The mirror of the great Chiavo," said Santora. He took a chair and put a parcel wrapped in white paper on the lamp table next to it. "A marvelous mirror!"

"Quite marvelous," said Mrs. Darnley. "Señor Santora, I've gone to a great deal of trouble to possess certain mirrors, but your persistence is ridiculous."

"It is not ridiculous to wish to own the Chiavo glass," said he. "Mrs. Darnley—señora—I would desire to speak with you alone."

"There's no need for that," she answered. "We have nothing to discuss."

"But yes, we have a thing to discuss." His voice went up and he hunched forward in his chair. He waited. No one in the room moved.

"I see," he said at last. "So we must have the audience. As you wish. Señora, I have made to you a generous offer for the mirror. Today I am even more generous. I will give you ten thousand dollars for the Chiavo glass, and I will add an item from my own collection." He held out the parcel to her. "It is a little hand mirror which was found in the ruins of Pompeii."

Mrs. Darnley laughed. "I have more money than I ever expect to spend, and things from Pompeii aren't so rare. But there is only one goblin glass."

"Only one," he agreed. "It is unique in all the world. Señora, I must have it!"

"No," she said.

"It is extremely important. You cannot understand

how important it is!" Santora cried.

"Of course it is important if it is the only one in the world. But it is just as important to me as to you. Why should your collection be better than mine?"

"Señora, I must warn you!" he said loudly. His hands were clenched, and Jupiter Jones saw Mrs. Darnley sit straighter in her chair.

"Of what?" she demanded. She stared into the man's face. "Señor Santora, do you know that today a man broke into this house? He was discovered here, in this very room."

The flush faded from Santora's face. Indeed, he went rather pale. He glanced at the mirror. "In this room? But . . . but no, how could I know that?"

"Let us hope that there is no way," she replied.

His gaze went to the floor, then to his own hands. "He was discovered? Here?" Santora raised his head and smiled a rather strained smile. "But of course. I read in your newspapers that you have thieves who come in the daytime to houses that are empty. I hope, señora, that your police will deal strictly with this man."

"Unfortunately, he got away," said Mrs. Darnley.

"I see." He frowned, as if thinking through some problem. "Señora, of this man who came into your house I can tell you nothing," he said. "We know that one man—one small man—cannot carry away the mirror of Chiavo, do we not? But there is danger in the glass."

"Oh?" said Mrs. Darnley.

"I have not been completely honest with you," said Santora. "I am not in truth a collector. The mirror from Pompeii—I purchased it yesterday from a dealer in Beverly Hills."

"I hope you didn't pay too much," she said, not unkindly.

"If it does not induce you to part with the Chiavo glass, perhaps I did. You see, it is not only that the Chiavo glass in unique in all the world. I am unique in all the world."

Mrs. Darnley was amused. "You don't appear to be *that* unusual, Señor Santora."

"I will tell you the story of the mirror," he said.

"But I know the story of the mirror."

"You only think you know." The anger was gone from his voice and his face now. He spoke softly, almost as if he were pleading. "Chiavo was a most great sorcerer. He had the glass fashioned to his order, and there were many spells which he said when the work was done. He could see through the glass into the world of the little ones, the spirits who dwell in the world under ours. And they told him many true things about events to come. And then, one day, Chiavo disappeared."

"I know that," said Mrs. Darnley. "And he left the glass with a family in Madrid, a family named Estancia."

Santora nodded. "So much is true, and much more than that. Chiavo had enemies—people who feared him and who said that he had harmed them. So he never let it be known that the family named Estancia was *his* family—his wife and his son. That son had a son, and that son had a daughter, and that daughter married, and so the name Estancia was lost. But always the family kept the glass. And then, more than forty years ago, before I was born, the glass of the great Chiavo was stolen. It was in Madrid. Oh, the thief, he paid for it most dearly. My father traced him and . . ."

"Your father?" cried Mrs. Darnley. "Do you mean to tell me that you are a descendant of Chiavo?"

He bowed. "The only one. My father is now dead. Only I am left, and I must have the glass. It is mine and I must leave it to my son."

Mrs. Darnley sat quietly. Her face was thoughtful.

"If your father traced the thief," she said at last, "when the mirror was stolen all those years ago, why didn't he get it back?"

"Because the thief was already dead and the glass had been taken by another scoundrel. You see, with us the mirror is safe. We know the secret. We know how to use it and, with the glass, we can know the future."

"A useful thing," said Mrs. Darnley.

"Indeed. But with people who are not of the Chiavo blood, there is danger. The man who stole it from my father was found in his house and he was dead. His only wound was a mark on his forehead that looked like a burn—but he was dead. And the mirror was gone. My father again tried to trace it.

Once he heard that it was in the possession of a man who lived in Barcelona. He went there, but too late. The man had hanged himself. The landlord of that man had taken the mirror from the room and sold it, and the man who bought it . . ."

"Did he hang himself too?" asked Mrs. Darnley.

"He died in a train wreck. He died before my father could get to him, and his son gave the mirror to a friend who was traveling to Madrid. The son said that before his father died, his father saw an image in the glass. He saw the image of a man with long white hair and eyes that were strange and green. It was the image of Chiavo, and my father was not surprised. You see, we who are of the family of Chiavo know where he went when he disappeared. He went into the mirror and beyond, to the dark places under the earth where the spirits live. He is there still, but sometimes he comes to the glass and he looks out, and this is for a warning."

Mrs. Darnley put her hand to her throat. "He went . . . through the looking glass?"

"Like Alice," said Jean. It was barely a whisper.

"I . . . I cannot believe that," said Mrs. Darnley.

"So you say now," declared Santora. "But you know the rest. The man who traveled to Madrid sold the glass to a student at the university, a student named Diego Manolos. Soon after, Manolos left Spain and returned to the place where he had been born. It is a place that you know, Señora Darnley, a tiny island of a country called Ruffino. There he married a lady who was your friend and who is still your friend. What does your friend say about the mirror?"

"She didn't like it," said Mrs. Darnley. "She thought it ugly, which it certainly is. She would have given it to me years ago, but her husband wouldn't part with it. But she never said she saw anything in the glass. Manolos had it for more than thirty years, and she never saw any spirit in it."

Santora leaned toward her and his voice was very low, so low that Jupe found himself straining to hear. "The glass is cursed," he said. "Chiavo curses any who possess it, unless they are of his blood."

"But Diego Manolos wasn't cursed," insisted Mrs. Darnley. "He was very successful. He was an adviser to the president of Ruffino."

"Perhaps the curse fell upon his wife," suggested Santora. His dark eyes were fixed upon Mrs. Darnley, unblinking. "Tell me, Señora Darnley, about your friend who married Manolos. Was she a happy woman?"

Mrs. Darnley turned her head away. "Well . . . no. I think Isabella Manolos was not a happy woman when her husband was alive. I think he always treated her badly. But now he is dead, and . . ."

"And the first thing his widow did after his death was to send you the mirror," Santora reminded her.

"She knew I wanted it." Mrs. Darnley shook herself as if waking from a bad dream, and she stood up. "Señor Santora, you have told me a tale which I cannot believe. No one can disappear into a mirror. But if you are indeed a descendant of Chiavo, there must be documents—records of births and marriages. If the mirror is really the property of your family, I will not keep it from you. But you must prove it."

Santora stood up, too, and took his parcel from the table. "It has taken many years to find the mirror," he said. "My father followed the trail from Madrid to Barcelona and back to Madrid. I followed it to Ruffino, and when I reached the widow of Manolos it was too late. Now I am here. It will take still more time to get the documents you ask for, but I have the time. I will send to Spain.

"I will wait," said Mrs. Darnley.

"Yes, señora, and while you wait, be careful. The glass is dangerous."

He went out of the library, and the boys heard the front door open, then close behind him.

"What a tale that was!" exclaimed Pete. He looked a bit shaky.

"A beautifully constructed scare story," said Jupiter Jones.

"He must have been lying," declared Mrs. Darnley. She spoke as if she were trying to convince herself. "He couldn't be a descendant of Chiavo and . . . and no one can disappear into a mirror. If he is really a descendant of Chiavo, why didn't he say so right away, when he first came here more than a week ago?"

"Perhaps," said Jupiter Jones, "it just occurred to him to mention it today."

4

Jupiter Scents a Mystery

Before they left the Darnley house, Jupiter Jones gave Mrs. Darnley one of the business cards of The Three Investigators. "Our telephone number is on the back of the card," he said. "If we can be of any assistance to you, we will be very pleased."

She took the card, almost absent-mindedly, and folded it in half. "No one can disappear into a mirror," she insisted again.

"I shouldn't think so," said Jupiter, "but it will be interesting to see what documents Señor Santora can produce to support his story."

She nodded and they left her standing in the entrance hall of her grand and gloomy house, her grandchildren beside her. She looked tired and a bit haggard in her antique finery. She was not quite the brave lady they had first met, bemused by her mirrors and playing at being Marie Antoinette.

"That place gives me the willies!" exclaimed Pete, when the salvage yard truck was under way.

Jupe didn't answer. He leaned against the side of the truck, wrapped his arms around his knees, and closed his eyes.

"What is it, Jupe?" asked Bob.

"I'm not sure," said Jupiter Jones. "It was something Santora said—something wrong."

"He said plenty wrong!" declared Pete. "I don't care what kind of magic spells you put on a mirror, don't tell me that anybody can go through the looking glass and stay there on the other side! And come back every once in a while to scare the life out of real people! Or . . . or whatever that spook is supposed to do."

"That wasn't what I meant," said Jupe. "I think we can write off Santora's tale as a legend, or perhaps something he made up to try to frighten Mrs. Darnley into giving up the glass."

"I know," said Bob. "It was the part about how it took him thirty years to locate the mirror. That doesn't make sense. A man who is advisor to the president of a republic isn't exactly in hiding. Diego Manolos had the mirror all that time and he must have been a public figure."

"Ruffino is not in the news a great deal, is it?" asked Jupiter. "What do you know about it?"

The other two were silent.

"An obscure country that doesn't make news. Possibly it *could* have taken all that time to locate the mirror. No, that isn't what bothers me. It was Santora's description of the burglar that makes me wonder. Remember, he said, 'We know that one man—one small man—cannot carry away the mirror of Chiavo, do we not?' But he didn't see the burglar, and no one had described the burglar to him. Yet he said, correctly, that the burglar was a small man."

Bob groaned. "You and your tape-recorder memory! But maybe that's just a way of talking. Any man would seem small if he had to handle that mirror. It's a monster! Do you think Santora's in on the housebreaking somehow?"

"He seemed genuinely surprised when he heard there had been a break-in," decided Jupe. "Also, he seemed to be alarmed. That break-in meant something to him. He assumed immediately that the burglar was interested in the mirror, though Mrs. Darnley hadn't quite said so. And only then did he claim to be a descendant of Chiavo's—as if he had to act fast and give every possible reason why he should have the mirror. No, I don't think Santora knew about the break-in until Mrs. Darnley told him, but I do think it's possible that he knows who the burglar is. At any rate, I'm fairly certain that we'll be hearing more about the mirror."

"I don't mind if we never hear of it again," said Pete.

Jupiter Jones smiled, and the smile was one that his two friends knew very well. He had scented a mystery, and he was eager to take hold of it and solve it. "We must be prepared," he announced. "It will take Santora at least a week to get any kind of documents from Spain. By that time we can be ready."

"With what?" asked Pete.

"Information," said Jupiter happily. "We need to know more about Ruffino. We need to know about Chiavo. From what Mrs. Darnley said, he must have been a famous magician. I have never heard of him. We'll get busy, and when the time's right we'll be ready to move."

Jupe's estimate of the time the boys had available proved to be accurate. Almost exactly one week after The Three Investigators had visited the Darnley house, Jeff Parkinson rode the city bus to Rocky Beach. It was midafternoon when the carrot-haired youth found The Jones Salvage Yard. Jupe was in his outdoor workshop making minor repairs on an old printing press which he had put together out of spare parts from the yard. Jupe straightened up when he saw Jeff and wiped his hands on a piece of rag.

"You've heard from Señor Santora?" he asked.

Jeff shook his head and sat down in Jupe's swivel chair. "Not a word," he said.

Pete wandered in. He had on a freshly laundered shirt and his hair was wet. "Hi!" he said, when he saw Jeff. "You're a long way from home."

"How's the surf?" Jupiter asked him.

"Too good." Pete pulled up a wooden crate and sat on it. "Those swells are really high. I got wiped out three times, so I figured I didn't need a broken neck."

Jeff laughed. "Worthington said once you don't like trouble. 'Master Pete prefers to avoid unnecessary vexation,' is the way he put it."

Pete laughed. "Vexation isn't exactly what happens when you hang around with Jupiter Jones. The things Jupe can think of are downright scary."

"Sometimes it's necessary to take risks to solve a mystery," said Jupiter.

It was true. In a far corner of The Jones Salvage Yard was an old, damaged mobile home trailer. It was all but forgotten by Uncle Titus and Aunt Mathilda, and heaps of junk sheltered it from curious eyes. Inside that battered trailer was Headquarters, where The Three Investigators had their office, their files and telephone, a compact but complete laboratory, and a photographic darkroom. When Jupiter, Pete, and Bob had first started their detective firm, there had not been much need for file cabinets, but now there were several, filled with Bob's careful notes on their cases. They showed that the team of young sleuths had a record which men many years their senior might envy. And they showed that there had been risks—many risks. Jupe was not one to hesitate at taking chances.

"I have a feeling," said Jupiter to Jeff, "that you came here to tell us something important."

"I'm not sure," said Jeff Parkinson. "You heard Santora's story about the old magician going through the looking glass to the land of the goblins?"

"Fantastic," said Jupe. "But what about it? You said you hadn't heard any more from Santora. I presume he has not yet presented any documents to your grandmother to prove his claim that he is a descendant of Chiavo's."

"No, he hasn't. If he can prove it, he'll get the mirror. My grandmother wants to do what's right, but she doesn't want to be a sucker. She won't give up the mirror just because Santora can spin a wild yarn. Now, last week you met John."

"John Chan? Your grandmother's houseman? What about him?"

"He's really a very calm guy," said Jeff. "He's been with Grandma several years and I've never seen him get upset about anything. He just minds his business and does the cooking, and when he's not busy he practices the guitar. He's a Harvard dropout. His father wanted him to be a lawyer, but he just wants to play classical guitar."

"So?" said Pete.

"So John, who never gets upset, is now hearing things—and . . . and maybe I am too."

Jupe and Pete waited.

"I heard a sound last night like, well, like somebody laughing. I got up and went downstairs. The front door was locked tight, the way it was when we went to bed. I turned on the lights in the living room and everything looked okay. I started to go back to bed and I got this impression, the way you do when you see something out of the corner of your eye. I thought somebody went into the library, or maybe that something had moved inside the library. So I went in there and turned on a light and there wasn't anything. But when I went back to the hall, there was John in his bathrobe and he was carrying a carving knife. I . . . I thought maybe he'd flipped or something. I mean, he had this funny look on his face and there was that knife. I was scared!"

"And then?" prompted Jupe.

"Then I said something dumb, like, 'Hi.' He said, 'Oh! It's only you.' We were standing there in the hall, staring at each other, when we both heard the laughing sound. It came from the library where that mirror is. John was in there like a shot and there still wasn't anybody there. No one. Nothing. Four walls and a lot of books and the mirror."

Pete rubbed his jaw. "You mean, you think maybe the mirror *is* haunted?" he asked.

"I don't know. I know I don't believe the house is haunted, even if some people say it is. It may be kind of creepy, but nothing strange has ever happened to Grandma or John, or to Jean and me, and we come from Chicago every summer to visit Grandma."

"It is an interesting house," said Jupiter Jones. "I've read several articles about it. Drakestar the magician had it built after he retired from the stage. Drakestar dabbled in spiritualism and he entertained his friends in the house by performing for them. He died there twelve years ago, and the people who bought the house from his estate claim that his ghost returned several times."

"They heard noises at night," said Jeff, "but Grandma's been there for ten years and she's never heard anything. She says they imagined it. But now John is hearing things and so am I. John doesn't believe in ghosts, but he's nervous. He told me he's sleeping with that carving knife next to his bed, just in case, and he told me not to breathe a word to Grandma. He doesn't want to upset her. But I think she's hearing things too."

"Did she say anything?" asked Pete.

"No, she didn't. But after I talked to John, I went back to bed. I woke up again later on. I heard Grandma's door open, so I looked out. She was standing at the top of the stairs looking down. I asked her if anything was the matter and she jumped. Then she said she'd felt a draft and I should go back to sleep. Now, Grandma's not bothered by drafts. She never complains about stuff like that. I think she heard something."

"Is she frightened?" asked Jupiter Jones.

"I don't know. She's not saying anything, but I know I heard something and I think she did. There's never been anything weird before, so it can't be the ghost of Drakestar. It must have something to do with that mirror. You guys are detectives. Could you find out more about the mirror? Grandma really doesn't know too much about it. Just what her friend told her."

"The widow of the man named Manolos," said Jupiter.

Jeff nodded. "When Grandma was very young, she

met a girl at boarding school who came from Ruffino. That's a little island country off the coast of South America, and some families there sent their children to the United States for school. After this girl graduated, she went back home and married Manolos. Grandma always kept in touch with her and even went to Ruffino a couple of times to see her. Grandma didn't like Manolos. She thought he was a real creep, and he was mean to her friend. Just the same, he got ahead in the world and he was an adviser to the president. When he died a month ago, Señora Manolos sent the glass to Grandma. We know that Manolos bought the mirror in Spain and that Chiavo was supposed to have used it when he talked with those ugly little goblins, but that's all we really know."

"We've been curious too," said Jupiter Jones, "and perhaps we can tell you more about Chiavo and the mirror shortly. Bob and I have spent several days trying to find some material on the man. The Rocky Beach Library has nothing. Neither does the library at U.C.L.A., or the big library in Los Angeles. This morning Bob went to Ruxton University. There is a professor of anthropology there, Dr. Barrister, who is also a great collector of stories on psychic phenomena. He was a great help to us in solving a previous mystery, the Case of the Singing Serpent. He may know something about Chiavo. When Bob gets back . . ."

"I am back." Bob had suddenly appeared at the entrance to the workshop. He leaned his bicycle against the fence which formed part of the enclosure. "Just in time too, I see. Hi, Jeff."

"You found out something?" said Jupiter.

"I sure did. Ruxton University's a terrific place. Our friend in the anthropology department has written a couple of papers on the Chiavo glass. According to the old tales about Chiavo, he was one very powerful sorcerer, and the glass really is magic. Also, the legends have it that Chiavo never died. He went through the mirror to join the earth spirits, just the way Señor Santora said he did."

The four boys in the workshop were silent, pondering the legend of an old sorcerer supposedly still living in an alien, inhuman world. Suddenly the light dimmed and grayed. Pete stirred and looked up. "I think we're going to have a storm," he said, and for some reason he whispered the words.

A light bulb flashed over the printing press.

"Oho!" said Jupiter Jones. He pulled aside a grating that leaned against a workbench near the press and vanished into a length of large corrugated pipe which the grating had concealed.

"What the . . . ?" said Jeff Parkinson.

The light over the press stopped flashing. Bob pointed to it. "That's the signal that the telephone's ringing in Headquarters. Jupe just went in through Tunnel Two and answered it. Does your grandmother know you're here?"

"My sister does," said Jeff.

"Then that could be her. Come on."

Jeff Parkinson went down on his hands and knees

and followed Bob and Pete through the pipe, which had been padded with odd pieces of carpeting. At the end was a trap door leading directly into the Headquarters of The Three Investigators. Jupiter was there, standing over the desk, the telephone to his ear.

"How long ago?" the others heard him ask.

Jeff climbed through the trap door and looked around. The office inside the mobile home trailer was crowded but orderly. Along with the desk, chairs, and files, Jeff noticed a microscope and some pieces of electronic equipment, which Jupe had devised to aid in detective work.

"I think you did the right thing," Jupiter was saying into the telephone. "We'll do anything we can. Keep the doors locked and wait."

He put down the telephone.

"What's up?" said Bob.

Jupe looked past Bob to Jeff. "That was your sister," he said. "She and your grandmother came home from a shopping trip about fifteen minutes ago and went upstairs. They heard someone laughing down in the library. They started down the stairs, and when they were halfway to the bottom they looked into the library and saw a man in the mirror. He was very pale and he had long white hair and very bright green eyes."

"Chiavo!" said Jeff.

"Mrs. Darnley wants an investigation, and she wants The Three Investigators to take the case! Worthington will pick us up in half an hour!"

5
Another Warning

Worthington was at the salvage yard in less than half an hour. He picked up the boys and drove as rapidly as the law allowed back to the Darnley house.

"I must return the Rolls to the auto rental agency," he told the boys as he let them out. "After that, I shall go directly home. Call me if I can be of help."

The Three Investigators promised that they would and followed Jeff to the door, which Jean opened before they could ring the bell. They went in to find Mrs. Darnley sitting in a small chair in the entrance hall, staring grimly into the library. She looked pale, and she did not move as Jean locked the front door.

"I can't quite bring myself to go in there," she said, "but I have made sure no one came out."

"Have you been watching those doors ever since you saw whatever was in the mirror?" asked Jupe.

"I haven't taken my eyes off them," said Mrs. Darnley. She raised a hand to her hair and the boys could see that it was shaking slightly.

"I called you and got Grandma a chair, and then I checked all the doors and windows," Jean reported.

"Where's John?" asked Pete.

"It's his day off," Jeff said.

"So the house was empty while you were out, Mrs. Darnley?" asked Jupe.

"Empty and locked. Dead-bolt locks on both doors and bars on every window. None of them was tampered with. No one could get in here. No one. And I know the doors were locked when we left. John left with us. I watched him lock up and then Jean checked to make sure the doors were secure."

"Is it possible that John came back later, and wasn't so careful?" said Jupiter.

"No. Several of the students in John's guitar class were giving a concert at the Ebell Club today and John was the featured performer. We dropped John off at the Ebell on our way to Westwood."

Jupiter stepped into the library. Mrs. Darnley hesitated for a moment, then got up and followed him. The room was almost dark. The day had become grey, and the heavy drapes on the windows were closed. Jupe saw his own shadowy image in the mirror. He switched on a table lamp and looked around. Bob and Pete came into the room, and Jean stood uncertainly on the threshold. The library looked as it had the week before. Nothing seemed out of place.

"Jean, where were you when you saw the ghost in the glass?" asked Jupe. "Do you remember the exact place?"

"I sure do." Jean turned and went out and part of the way up the staircase. She stood still, frowning, about eight steps from the top. "Here," she called. "I was here and Grandma was a step or two below me."

"All right. Stay there." Jupe retreated to the far corner of the library, keeping his eyes fixed on the mirror. When he found a spot where he could stand and see Jean's reflection in the glass, he called, "Can you see me?"

"I can see you in the mirror," she called back.

"That's how it could have been done," said Jupiter to Mrs. Darnley. "If someone stood right here, where I am now, you would have seen his reflection as you came down the stairs, and it would appear that he was an apparition in the mirror. This room is fairly dark, with those drapes drawn. Did you see him clearly?"

Mrs. Darnley closed her eyes as if she did not want to think of it. "Very clearly. He . . . well, kind of glowed."

"A secret exit!" cried Bob. "There has to be another way out of the room!"

"Unless . . . unless there *is* a ghost," said Pete, shivering.

The boys searched then. Pete and Jeff turned back the carpets and examined the floor, probing at cracks with a kitchen knife. Bob and Jupe took books off the shelves and rapped at the walls behind the shelving.

"It sounds solid," said Bob. "I can tell where the studs are."

Jupe scowled. He pointed to the wall opposite the mirror. "What's next to this room?" he asked.

"Nothing," said Mrs. Darnley. "That's an outside wall. The hillside slopes up there. In fact, part of that wall is beneath ground level. That's why there aren't any windows there, or on the north wall of the living room."

"Hmm!" Jupe scowled and pulled at his lip. He rapped at the wall again. "I can't believe it," he said.

The doorbell sounded in the entrance hall and they all jumped.

"I'll get it," said Jean.

Mrs. Darnley and the boys heard her struggle with the locks on the door, then say, "Oh, it's you."

Almost immediately, Señor Santora came into the library. Jean was close behind him and she was angry.

"I didn't ask you to come in!" she said.

Señor Santora scowled at the boys. He glanced at the turned-back carpets and at the books piled on the floor. "Ah!" he said. Jupe thought that there was a note of satisfaction in his voice.

"You've come to tell us something?" asked Mrs. Darnley.

"I have come to see that my mirror is safe. I still await the documents from Spain. But something has happened here. You have had, I think, a fright."

"Nothing has happened," said Mrs. Darnley evenly.

"You have seen something," he insisted. "I think you have seen Chiavo. Señora, do not delay or it may be too late. To see Chiavo is a warning. Let me take the glass."

"If you can prove that you are the rightful owner," said Mrs. Darnley, "then you may take the glass."

"As you wish." He took out a small notebook and wrote something in it with a silver pencil. He tore the page from the book and handed it to Mrs. Darnley. "You may change your mind," he said. "If you do, please call me at my hotel. In case you have forgotten, it is the Beverly Sunset. Here is the number."

He bowed and went out, and Jean locked the front door behind him.

"He knew!" said Mrs. Darnley. "He knew we saw that thing in the mirror. How could he have known?"

"Perhaps he knew, Mrs. Darnley," said Jupiter Jones, "or perhaps he was only guessing. Certainly he had to be aware that *something* had transpired. Why else would we have the room in such an upset state?"

Mrs. Darnley glanced at the telephone number Santora had given her. "Señor Santora is running up quite a hotel bill for the sake of my mirror. The Beverly Sunset isn't cheap. My friend Emily Stonehurst used to live there."

"I think I know the place," said Jupe. "It's on the south side of Sunset Boulevard, isn't it? Just west of the Sunset Strip?"

"That's right. The corner of Sunset and Rosewood."

"Bob and Pete," said Jupe, "Worthington told us he'd be at home if we needed him. Why don't you call him and ask if he'll drive you to that hotel so you can keep an eye on Señor Santora? Doubtless there is a service entrance as well as the main entrance, so it will take two."

"Okay! I'll be glad to get out of here," said Pete quickly.

"I guess I can call my mother and tell her I won't be home for dinner," said Bob. "What are you going to do while we're watching Santora?"

The stocky First Investigator fingered the weird moldings which decorated the goblin glass. "Jeff and I can put the books back on the shelves," he said, "and then we can wait. It will be interesting to know if the ghost of Chiavo will appear while you have Santora under surveillance."

6

Pete Stalks Trouble

Pete, Bob, and Worthington had paused only for a hasty snack at a hamburger stand on their way to Beverly Hills. It was dusk and storm clouds were piling up in the sky north of the mountains when they reached the Beverly Sunset Hotel. The handsome four-story brick building occupied a whole block on Sunset Boulevard.

"It looks expensive," said Pete.

Worthington parked his Ford sedan in the block beyond the hotel, across the boulevard from it. "It *is* considered a desirable place," he said. "I have driven several people who were guests there. It isn't an ordinary commercial hotel, and it attracts few visitors from out of the city. Some guests are permanent residents who don't want the responsibilities that go with maintaining a home."

"I guess we can conclude that Señor Santora isn't hurting for money," said Bob.

"There he is now!" said Pete.

The three in the car watched intently as the gentleman from Spain came out of the hotel. He stood for a moment looking at the clouds and listening to far-off thunder, then turned away from the boys and strolled down the sidewalk, hands in his pockets.

Worthington frowned. "Dare I make a U-turn on Sunset?"

Señor Santora paused and examined the display in the window of a flower shop, then ambled on for a few hundred yards, paused again, stared into the window of an art supply house, and after a moment, went into the shop.

"I don't think he's going anywhere," said Pete. "I think he's just killing time."

"Hey!" said Bob suddenly. "Look! There at the corner!"

A thin man dressed in a dark, somewhat rumpled suit had come around a corner onto the boulevard and was walking rapidly toward the entrance of the hotel.

"It's the burglar!" said Pete.

"Indeed it is, Master Pete." Worthington made a move as if to get out of the car.

"Hold it, Worthington," warned Pete quickly. "This may be our big chance to find out what's up."

"The man is a criminal," Worthington pointed out. "He broke into Mrs. Darnley's house."

"I know, I know," said Pete. "And Mrs. Darnley thinks that Santora might have put him up to it. And now, just after that weird thing appeared in the mirror, here he is at Santora's hotel."

Pete frowned, thought for a few moments, then sighed and slowly began to get out of the car.

"What are you going to do?" asked Bob.

"Follow him," said Pete. "What else can I do? If he and Santora are in cahoots we've got to know about it."

"If they're going to meet in that art shop you'd better be careful," said Bob. "They've both seen you before. They'll recognize you."

"That housebreaker could be dangerous," warned Worthington.

Pete's face was grim. "I know it," he said. "Don't worry. I'll be careful."

He hurried down to the intersection, keeping his eyes on the black-clad figure. The burglar was walking with his head down so that his eyes were fixed on the pavement in front of him. To Pete's relief, he did not proceed toward the art shop. He went into the hotel.

Pete crossed the boulevard when the light changed. He walked toward the hotel with his head up and his lips pursed as if he were whistling—a young man with not a serious thought in his head. And he went into the hotel after the burglar.

The lobby of the Beverly Sunset was quiet and thickly carpeted. There were low, round tables with

fresh-cut flowers on them, numbers of deep, uphol-
stered sofas and chairs, and a scattering of elderly
ladies and gentlemen, some simply sitting, some read-
ing or quietly chatting.

Pete spotted his quarry immediately. The dark-
suited housebreaker was on in the far side of the
lobby, talking to the desk clerk.

Pete tried to imagine what Jupiter Jones would do
under the circumstances, and decided that Jupiter
would certainly attempt to eavesdrop on the conver-
sation at the desk. He went noiselessly across the carpeted floor, stopped about four feet from the housebreaker, went down on one knee and began to fumble
with his shoelaces.

"I am sorry, sir," said the desk clerk. "Señor Santora is not in at the moment."

"Then I will leave a message," said the dark man.
"Some paper, if you please?"

"Certainly, sir."

Pete stood up to see the burglar bent over the desk,
writing something. Pete looked at the clock over the
desk, checked it against his own wristwatch, turned
away, and sat down on one of the sofas, his back to
the desk.

"There," said the burglar. "You will see that Señor
Santora receives this?"

"Of course," answered the clerk.

Pete sneaked a look over his shoulder. The dark,
thin man was still standing with his back to Pete. Pete
watched the desk clerk put a folded piece of paper

into a numbered slot behind the desk. The number on the slot was 426.

The desk clerk finished this small task, then faced the thin visitor and raised an eyebrow, as if to ask if anything more were required at the moment.

"It is most important," said the man.

"I will watch for Señor Santora," promised the clerk.

Behind the desk a telephone buzzed.

"If you'll excuse me," murmured the clerk. He turned away and picked up the telephone.

The thin man sidled away and slipped around a corner into a corridor where a sign pointed the way to the elevators. An instant later Pete heard an elevator door close, and then a hum which told him that the elevator car was in motion. Señor Santora's visitor was not going to rely on the desk clerk to deliver his message! Pete realized that the message was probably only a ruse—a trick to get the hotel clerk to put something in Santora's mailbox so that the burglar would know Santora's room number.

Pete hesitated a moment, then got to his feet and walked slowly past the desk and around the corner into the corridor where the elevators were located.

There were two elevators and there was also a stairwell, closed off by a heavy steel fire door. Again Pete paused, feeling the muscles in his stomach tighten. Then he opened the door and went up, taking the steps two at a time. When he reached the fourth floor landing he eased the fire door open a few inches and peered nervously into the hallway.

He saw the luxurious carpeting of the lobby re-peated. He saw small, low tables set against walls, and more masses of fresh flowers, and he saw doors. Doors and doors and more doors. But he did not see the slim, dark stranger.

Pete stepped out of the stairwell into the hallway and walked down the hall until he came to Room 426. He felt completely bewildered. Was the burglar in Santora's room? Was he about to rob Santora? Or was he waiting to talk to Santora? Should Pete get help?

He looked up and down the hall. There was no tele-phone. There was only the carpeting, the tables and the flowers, and the blank, closed doors. Should he run back to the lobby and alert the desk clerk?

Again, Pete tried to imagine he was Jupiter Jones. Would Jupe run back to the lobby? No, Pete decided. Jupe would stay put and see what happened. He could always follow the burglar if the man left before Santora returned. And if Santora returned before the man left, there might be some interesting events to observe.

But he could not linger in the hall. If one of the numbered doors opened—if one of the hotel guests stepped into the corridor—he would surely be ques-tioned. He had to get out of sight.

Almost directly across from Santora's room there was a door that had no number. Pete tried the knob. It turned. He pulled the door open and smelled wax and dampness. He had found the broom closet.

"Nice going," Pete told himself. He stepped into the closet, careful not to disturb the brooms and mops leaning against the wall, or to stumble over the vacuum cleaner. He closed the door, all but an inch or two, leaned against a shelf that held an assortment of soap and furniture polish, and peeked out through the crack between the door and the doorjamb. He grinned. He could see Santora's door. And if anyone opened that door he would be able to see right into Santora's room.

He waited, not moving. The sound of thunder reached him from outside.

Down the hall, the elevator hummed, then stopped. Pete heard the door slide open. Footsteps sounded slightly on the carpeted floor. A man was coming toward Pete, walking heavily. Pete heard something muttered in Spanish. Then he saw Señor Santora pass the broom closet, stop at the door of Room 426, and put a key into the lock.

Pete opened the closet door another inch, anxious not to miss one thing that might happen.

Santora frowned, turned the key twice, then pushed open the door to his room. He went in and closed the door behind him. Pete slipped out of the closet, stepped across the hall, and was about to apply his ear to the panels of the door to 426 when he heard something that froze him like a statue. He heard the sound of a blow, then the heavier sound of someone falling!

The door of Santora's room opened. For a single tick of a clock, Pete and the black-clad burglar stared at one another.

"You!" snarled the burglar. He rushed at Pete.

Pete dodged, and the man's charge carried him past Pete. He crashed into the wall across from 426. It seemed to Pete that he fairly bounced off the wall. Then he was running down the hall toward the stairs and Pete saw that he had something white crumpled in one hand.

Pete dived for the man's legs. He connected. The man sprawled on his face and the white thing he carried bounced away. He kicked, thrashed, twisted, and at last managed to bring his fist down on top of Pete's head.

Pete felt his senses slip away for a moment. The man scrambled up and ran, and the door to the stairwell banged.

Pete managed to stand up, trembling. He leaned against the wall. His gaze blurred, then cleared and focused on that white crumpled thing the man had carried. It lay on the edge of the carpeting near the wall. Almost without thinking, Pete picked it up and stuffed it into his pocket.

He went back to Room 426. The door stood open and Pete saw Señor Santora sprawled on the floor. Blood trickled from behind his ear and ran down his neck, staining his collar.

"Migosh!" Pete took four quick strides, reached Santora, and knelt over him. His fingers searched for the man's pulse, and he sighed with relief when he

found it. Santora might be seriously injured, but he was not dead.

There was a telephone on a desk amid a pile of papers that had been spilled from an open attaché case. Pete picked up the telephone.

"Can I help you?" said the pleasant voice of the hotel operator.

"Señor Santora has been hurt," said Pete quickly. "Get the police and get a doctor here right away!"

Before the startled operator could answer, Pete had the telephone back in the cradle. He stepped over Santora and dashed down the corridor to the stairwell. As he went down the stairs he heard the elevator again. It was coming up from the lobby.

Pete reached the first floor and stepped out into the corridor. He forced himself to walk calmly across the lobby. There seemed to be no excitement here but the clerk was not at the desk.

Pete went on out to the boulevard. It was quite dark now and the rain had begun. Thunder grumbled and rolled, and lightning flickered above the hills. Pete hurried, hunching himself against the rain. When the traffic signal at the corner changed, he ran across to the car where Worthington and Bob were waiting. Snatching the door open, he flung himself into the back seat.

"What happened?" asked Bob. "We saw Santora go back into the hotel. Did he meet the burglar?"

Pete didn't answer right away. He only stared down at his hands. They were trembling.

"What is it?" asked Bob.

"Did you . . . did you see that crook come out?" asked Pete shakily.

"No. Isn't he with Santora?"

Pete shook his head. "I . . . I called the desk clerk," he said. "That little guy . . . he must have gotten out through the service door."

"Master Pete, what happened?" said Worthington.

A siren wailed down the boulevard and a police car screamed its way through traffic and drew up at the front of the hotel.

"The burglar," said Pete. "He tried to kill Santora. At least, he hit him an awful wallop. I didn't hang around. I . . . I couldn't. I mean, it would look really bad if they found me in that room. Santora—he was bleeding all over the place!"

7

The Ghost in the Glass

After Bob and Pete left the Darnley house with Worthington, Jupiter Jones prowled through the mansion making sure that the doors were locked and bolted, that the grillwork on the windows was secure. He roamed the shadowy rooms, trying to ignore the sensation that there was motion all about him—motion on every side, as if the old house pulsed with a sinister life of its own. He reminded himself, again and again, that it was all the result of the mirrors— mirrors everywhere in which only his own reflection moved.

Then he stood in the library and listened. He could hear Jean and Mrs. Darnley in the kitchen at the other end of the house. They were clattering about, putting dishes on the table there. The refrigerator door slammed and the exhaust fan over the stove hummed. These were simple, everyday sounds, comforting and warm. Yet they seemed alien in this place where, in spite of locks and bars and solid walls, someone or something appeared at will.

Thunder rumbled far off to the north, and there was another shadow in the goblin glass. It was Jeff Parkinson; he had come into the library.

"It'll be dark early tonight," said Jeff.

"Yes," said Jupe. "Unless the storm blows over."

Jeff's face was a bit pinched. He spoke as if straining for some ordinary remark. "I thought it didn't rain in California in the summertime."

"It doesn't often," said Jupiter Jones.

"Grandma's got supper ready," said Jeff. "We're going to eat in the kitchen. There aren't any mirrors there. I think right now she doesn't want to see any more mirrors."

Jupe nodded and followed Jeff down the long corridor, past Mrs. Darnley's carefully arranged settings for her treasured mirrors, and into the big, brightly lighted kitchen. John Chan was not expected to return to the house until morning, and a bureau had been shoved in front of the door that led from the kitchen out to the garage.

Mrs. Darnley had been wearing a light summer suit when she returned from her shopping trip with Jean. Now she had on slacks and a shirt that managed to be perfectly plain and at the same time extremely expensive-looking. Her silver-gold hair was pulled back and pinned up in a knot at the nape of her neck.

"We won't see any ghost here," she said. She put a platter of scrambled eggs down on the table. "I think I'm glad that John won't let me put mirrors in the kitchen."

"You've seen an apparition in only one looking glass," Jupe reminded her. "The Chiavo glass."

She sat down. At that moment she appeared tired and old and somewhat wasted. "Sometimes," she said, "I think that all of my mirrors are haunted. Sometimes, when I'm alone, when you children aren't here, I feel as if *I'm* the ghost."

Jupiter Jones felt a sudden stirring of alarm. Had his client become so involved with her world of mirrors that the real world was slipping away from her? "Mrs. Darnley," he said quickly, "you never *have* seen a ghost in any mirror before?" he asked.

She looked at him and her expression, which had been absently dreamy, sharpened. She smiled. "No, Jupiter. I haven't. But in this house I see myself coming and going more often than anyone needs to, and I guess I think too much about those others—the tragic ones who have also seen themselves in the mirrors. Nonetheless, I do not have hallucinations. I have never before seen a specter in a glass."

"Good," said Jupiter. "Then we have only that one mirror to consider—the Chiavo glass. Mrs. Darnley, either that mirror is really haunted, or there is a way to enter this house which you don't know about, or there is someone hidden here in a place we can't find. It has to be one of those three things."

Mrs. Darnley nodded. "Yes, I know."

"Most of the disturbing noises that have been heard in the past week have been heard at night, haven't they?" asked Jupiter.

"Yes," said Mrs. Darnley. "The first time I saw the ghost . . ."

Jupe stiffened. "You saw it before today?"

"I saw it last night," she admitted. "It was late. It was very late. I'd heard Jeff and John prowling around, and after they went back to bed I couldn't sleep. Then, after a long time, I heard someone walking in the corridor. I got up. I knew it wasn't Jeff because I can hear Jeff's door open, no matter how careful he tries to be. I knew it wasn't John. I know John's walk. I put on a robe and went out into the hall. It was dark, of course, but not so dark that I couldn't see anything. There wasn't anybody in the hall, but there was a noise, a horrible little giggle. It seemed to be coming from the library. I went to the top of the stairs and started down, and well, I saw pretty much what Jean and I saw this afternoon—a face. That awful face in the mirror."

"The library was dark this afternoon with the drapes drawn," said Jupiter. "Last night it must have been even darker."

"Completely," said Mrs. Darnley. "Just the same, I saw that face."

"Grandma, why didn't you say something?" demanded Jeff. "I was right there. Why didn't you tell me?"

"Because I do not believe in ghosts," declared Mrs. Darnley. "I was not about to say I'd seen one. But today, when Jean saw it too, I had to admit it."

"Very well," said Jupe. "Here's what I suggest we do. Everyone go upstairs. Early. Right now. Do you have a television upstairs?" Mrs. Darnley nodded. "Good. We can all watch television."

"All of us?" said Jean.

"Not quite," said Jupiter. "We'll put out the lights in the hall and I'll sit on the stairs, in the place where you stood this afternoon, Mrs. Darnley, when you and Jean saw the ghost. Perhaps, when the house is quiet, the spirit of Chiavo will come back. Perhaps we can discover how the image appears in the mirror."

The idea was a good one. After they had eaten, Jean, Jeff, and Mrs. Darnley trooped noisily up the stairs. Mrs. Darnley inquired loudly as to Jupiter's choice of television shows. And as Mrs. Darnley put out the lights in the upstairs hall, Jupe took his post on the stairway facing the open library doors.

For perhaps half an hour there was no sound except for the noise of the approaching storm and subdued laughter from the TV. Lightning flickered occasionally, and thunder sounded near, then far away, then near again. Jupe waited, not daring to let himself relax even for a moment.

Then he heard a slight noise below. It was so faint that he couldn't be sure he *had* heard it. It was a tiny wail, or perhaps only a squeak. Was it the timbers protesting the drop in temperature, or had something moved?

There was a thud!

Jupe started. There was no mistaking that. It was a heavy sound, as if someone had dropped something —or perhaps as if someone had stamped.

Still Jupe saw nothing. There was the outline of the library doorway, a black oblong in the darkened hall. Beyond that there was nothing.

Something laughed. Though he didn't frighten easily, Jupe shivered. The laugh was nasty, mocking, almost the laugh of a demented being.

A greenish light flickered in the library, and suddenly—so suddenly that he blinked—Jupiter found himself staring down through the doorway and into the hideous mirror. He was staring at the ghost!

Jupiter froze for an instant, horrified! The thing in the glass vanished, and Jupe rubbed his eyes. He could hardly believe he had seen it. The hair was gray and matted, straggling down either side of the face like dank seaweed. The face was paler than chalk, whiter than death, and it glowed as if lit by some unearthly power. And the eyes—the eyes were wide, green, glittering, mocking eyes!

Down the hall, the door to the television room opened.

Again Jupe heard the laughter, and saw the greenish light and the hideous face in the mirror.

Jupe lunged to his feet and stumbled down the stairs. Suddenly the thing in the mirror vanished. There was only darkness. The mocking laughter sounded again, fainter, fading away.

Jupe skidded across the hallway into the library

and scrabbled wildly for a light. His hands touched a lamp and the switch clicked.

The library was empty. Except for Jupe himself, and his own white-faced reflection in the goblin glass, there was no one in the room.

8

The Phantom's Den

Jeff Parkinson's reflection appeared suddenly in the glass beside Jupiter's.

"You saw it?" said Jeff.

Jupe nodded.

Jean and Mrs. Darnley crowded through the doorway behind Jeff. Mrs. Darnley took one look at Jupe's white face and gave out a sound that was half laugh, half sigh. "It was terrible, wasn't it?" she said.

Jupiter Jones took a deep breath and willed his hands not to tremble. He managed to say, calmly enough, "It was very dreadful. I do not blame you, Mrs. Darnley, for not wanting to admit you saw it."

But then Jupe looked around at the bare walls, and at the mirror. "But where did it go?" he demanded.

"Back where it came from, let's hope," said Jean. She shivered. "Maybe . . . maybe the story Señor

Santora told is true. Maybe Chiavo does appear in the glass."

"But . . . but that's impossible," said Mrs. Darnley. "People don't really exist in mirrors, do they? That's only a mirror. An ordinary mirror. Except for the frame, of course, which is a monstrosity."

"Yes." Jupe went to the mirror and touched the frame. "A monstrosity, but an ordinary monstrosity. A solid steel frame. No wires. No way for it to play tricks. Nothing odd about the glass itself, except that it's an antique. It showed us the image of a terrible old man. There *was* something in this room! There had to be. I saw it!"

The storm which had been threatening now broke with great fury. It seemed as if even the weather was protesting the dreadful presence in the mirror. There were the first few giant raindrops, then a gushing torrent, a sharp flare of lightning and then a clap of thunder that seemed to shake the old mansion to its foundations. The lamp blinked and went out.

"Oh dear!" said Mrs. Darnley. "That must have hit the power lines!"

Jupiter Jones stood in the blackness of the library, listening to the rain roar outside and carefully scanning the room. Suddenly his eyes were caught by a faint, gray-green glow that seemed to linger in midair near a back corner of the room.

Jupe walked toward that mysterious glow. He put out a hand in the darkness and touched it. He felt the edge of a bookshelf, and he felt something else—

something sticky. And when he took his hand away from the bookshelf his fingertips were faintly luminous.

"We need some light," he said.

Jean and Jeff went out, and Jupe heard them fumbling their way through the blackness of the house. Then there was light—the soft light of candles. "The batteries in the flashlight are dead," said Jeff. He put one candle down on a table and carried a second one to Jupe. "This is the best we can do."

Jupe looked at his hand. The greenish glow was gone. His fingers were smudged with some gray substance.

"What is it?" asked Jeff.

Jupe sniffed at the stuff, then turned to face Jean and Mrs. Darnley. "We are dealing with a ghost who wears makeup!" he announced. "Not the usual makeup, but one which glows in the dark. I think we will need more candles."

Jean brought more and lighted them, and Jupe scrutinized the shelf where a bit of the grayish stain remained. He wiped his hand on his handkerchief, took the books off the shelf, and glared at the wall behind the shelving. And he rapped and listened and rapped again.

"It sounds so solid," he said. "It's hard to believe, but there must be a door here. And this is an exterior wall at the back of the house. There could be a door to the outside. That could be the way the ghost has been coming and going in spite of all the locks and bolts and bars. There *has* to be a secret exit!"

"But the house is built into the hillside," said Mrs. Darnley. "There's solid earth on the other side of that wall."

"There could be a tunnel," said Jupiter Jones. "It wouldn't have to be large."

"Or another room." Jean pointed to the wall and her voice trembled. "Maybe that . . . that thing is standing there listening to us."

Jeff abruptly charged out of the library. Jupe heard him race to the kitchen. Drawers and cupboards were opened and shut. Then Jeff came back carrying a heavy wooden mallet. "I don't know what John uses this for," he said, "but I know what I'm going to do with it if that thing comes out of the wall."

"He may not be in the house now," said Jupiter Jones. "There's only one way to find out. We must discover how to open the door which I am sure is here."

Mrs. Darnley sat down. "Jupiter, please be careful."

"I am always careful," said Jupiter Jones.

He went about his search in his usual methodical manner. Jean and Jeff helped him take books down and poke and pry and twist and tap. For a while the task seemed futile. The wall behind the bookshelves showed no cracks or seams. The baseboard was solid and immovable. The light switches were simply light switches, complete with the proper wires which were visible when Jupiter unscrewed the switch plates.

Nothing turned, twisted, or gave way under probing fingers.

"There has to be a latch," said Jupe at last. "There must be a latch and it must be on this wall, but where?"

"Maybe it only opens from the other side," said Jeff.

"No. Remember, Drakestar the magician had this house built. That door, however it opens, had to be built to his order. Now, Drakestar was one of the greatest magicians, and his most famous feat was a disappearing trick. Even after he retired, he would invite people to dinner here and perform his disappearing trick for them. Tonight the ghost of Chiavo disappeared from this room. This must be the room Drakestar used when he entertained his guests, and that means that there must be a way to open the door from this side."

Jupe stared at the bookshelves. "Oh!" he said suddenly.

"What?" asked Jean.

"If nothing else works, the only thing we haven't tried has to be the thing that will work. Those bookshelves are very sturdy. Were they here when you bought the house, Mrs. Darnley?"

"Yes, they're built in."

"And you have kept them well filled with books. Now, nothing happens when we press down on a shelf, but suppose we do this." Jupe put his hand under the shelf where the smudge of makeup still showed and pushed up.

There was no sound, but there was a faint draft that made the candle flames dance. A section of the wall, shelving and all, swung away from the base-board.

No one in the room moved for a moment. All four stared at the opening in the wall. But no fearful being rushed out at them. They saw only a space, barely two feet wide. The far wall of the space was lined with concrete blocks which had to be the true exterior wall of the house.

Jupe felt Jeff close behind him as he looked into the narrow compartment between the walls. He saw dust and cobwebs, and then he saw stairs. They went down into inky darkness.

"A candle," said Jupe. "Hand me a candle."

Jeff got him one. Jupe paused for a second to ex-amine the section of the wall which had opened. "No wonder it sounded so solid," he said. "It's made of lathe and plaster just like any well-built wall, but it's hung on a steel frame. What a masterpiece!"

Jeff looked past Jupe and down the stairs into the blackness below. "Are you going down?" he whis-pered.

"You are most certainly not going down there!" cried Mrs. Darnley.

"I am sorry, but I think I must," said Jupiter. "I am somewhat averse to solving only part of a puzzle."

"Then I'm going with you!" announced Jeff.

"Jeff! Don't!" Mrs. Darnley's voice was shrill.

"Mrs. Darnley, the phantom may not be down there," Jupe pointed out. "He may be out of the house and away." Jupe stepped over the baseboard onto the stairs. Jeff clutched his mallet and followed.

The hidden stairway was steep. The guttering, wavering candle flame threw light on dusty, mildewed walls. Jupe smelled the sick-sour odor of age and dampness and of air confined for so long that it seemed dead.

The stairway suddenly made a sharp turn, ran down three more steep steps, and ended in a tiny cellar—a room made of concrete blocks and floored with cement. Jupe held his candle high and Jeff stood beside him.

"Nobody!" breathed Jeff. His voice was scarcely a whisper.

"But he *was* here," said Jupiter Jones softly. "See where the dust has been disturbed on the floor?"

The two boys crept away from the staircase. Jupe pointed at a pair of very old, battered trunks. He put his fingers to his lips to warn Jeff not to speak, then handed the candle to Jeff and bent to examine the nearest of the trunks. It was unlocked. The rusty latch hung free. Jupiter tugged at the lid, and it came up with a squeak of ancient hinges. Jeff held the candle closer and the boys saw a well-worn sleeping bag, some odd bottles and jars, and a sandwich wrapped in clear plastic.

Jupiter looked at Jeff. Jeff's eyes were wide and questioning. Jupe raised an eyebrow and pointed to the second trunk, which stood against the far wall. Jeff nodded. Yes, the ghost had lived here for some time, and might still be here. It was a large enough trunk. Jupe started toward it, walking on silent feet. Jeff held the candle high and gripped his mallet as Jupe reached toward the lid of the second trunk.

Before Jupe could touch it, the trunk lid flew up. There was the crash of the lid striking the wall. There was a scream. There was a confusion of sudden movement, and Jupe found himself staring into glittering green eyes. For a split second, there in the close little basement room, the boys saw the ghastly face of the magician Chiavo.

Then the hideous being rushed forward. Jupe was shoved back against Jeff. The candle dropped and went out as both boys fell down. The ghost glowed in the dark above them. Jeff gasped, and his mallet clattered on the floor. Jupiter grabbed at the phantom's long robe. It tore as the creature ran for the stairway.

Steps pounded on the stairs. Jupe rolled over. He had something in his hands—something soft. A piece of cloth. He jumped up and groped for the stairs. He had just found the bottom steps when he heard Jean Parkinson scream.

There was lightning then. Even in the little cellar room Jupe saw the reflected flash, and he saw the ghost clearly—a tall, lank, wild-haired creature. It was at the head of the steps, at the secret door. Jean screamed again.

Jupe got to the top of the stairs and through the library in time to see the ghost wrench open the locks

on the front door, swing the door wide, and race out into the storm. A glare of lightning showed a gaunt figure with streaming gray locks. There was a clap of thunder and the phantom vanished into the darkness.

"Dear heavens!" cried Mrs. Darnley.

Jupiter was breathing hard, but he was smiling. "A most interesting spirit," he said. "I have a piece of his robe!"

9

A Mysterious Letter

It was well after eight when Bob, Pete, and Worthington returned to the Darnley house. Jupe and Jeff were rummaging through the trunks in the secret room, Jean was standing guard at the front door, and Mrs. Darnley was vainly trying to get a dial tone on the telephone so that she could call the police.

"We almost caught the ghost of Chiavo," Jean told the boys. "He's been living in our basement. Come and look."

She led the way to the library, where the secret door stood open, and called down to Jupiter and Jeff. They came up the narrow hidden stairs considerably more dusty than they had been earlier in the evening. Jupe, however, had a cheerful air.

"I knew it couldn't be a ghost," he announced. "Somebody's been hiding out in a secret room under this one! How he got in I don't know. He's been living on cold canned beans, stale sandwiches, and bottled water. Ugh! And we found an old sleeping bag—also a mirror, an electric torch, and the makeup he used so he'd glow in the dark."

Mrs. Darnley, exasperated, came in from the hall. "I can't call the police. That storm must have taken out the telephone lines too."

"Well, there's no hurry, is there, Grandma?" asked Jean. "The spook is gone, whoever he is, and at least we know it wasn't Señor Santora or the skinny guy who broke in here. The ghost who went out the front door was much too tall to be either of them."

"When . . . how did the ghost go out the front door?" asked Pete. "Didn't you try to stop him?"

"About twenty minutes ago," said Jeff Parkinson. "We wanted to stop him, Jupe and I. I had this mallet, you see, and I was going to bop him a good one only . . . only he came out of that trunk down in the cellar like some kind of a screaming nightmare and I . . . I panicked."

"It was real spooky," Jean put in. "I knew something weird might come busting out of that room and I thought I was ready for it, but I screamed. Jupe's the only one who managed to do anything. He grabbed a hunk of the robe the man was wearing, and tomorrow he's going to try to find out where it came from."

"It's a very unusual material," Jupe told the others as he pulled the piece of cloth from his pocket.

"Heavy black wool with a lot of silver threads. Very theatrical. It may turn out to be a most valuable clue to the identity of our mysterious ghost. And what have you to report?"

"Santora's in the hospital," said Pete, "and that little guy we thought might have been hired by him to burgle this place and swipe the mirror is *not* his confederate." Pete then reported, as briefly as possible, what had happened at the Beverly Sunset Hotel. "After the burglar whopped Santora on the head, he went down the stairs and probably out the service entrance. Worthington and Bob were watching out in front and they didn't see him leave. We waited and watched until an ambulance came and took Santora away."

"I could kick myself," said Bob bitterly. "I should have been at that service entrance. Worthington could have kept an eye on the front door. We might have been able to trail that guy, or at least get his license number."

"It was exceedingly remiss of us," said Worthington. "However, both Master Robert and I assumed that the man planned to meet with Señor Santora. We felt no need to watch for his departure from the hotel, especially after we saw Señor Santora return."

"You're not the only one to have a clue, though," Pete told Jupiter. He took a crumpled piece of paper from his pocket. "The burglar dropped this in the hallway. I can't read it. It's not in English. But if that guy wanted it, it must be important. It's a letter, and,

Mrs. Darnley, your name is mentioned."

"Oh?" Mrs. Darnley sat down.

The lights suddenly went on.

"Well, thank goodness for that," said Mrs. Darnley. "Jean, put out these candles before we burn the place down and let's see what's in that paper Pete picked up." She glanced at it, then looked around. "Does anybody here read Spanish or Portuguese?"

"I know a little Spanish, Mrs. Darnley," said Jupiter. He took the paper and read it through, frowning and pulling at his lower lip as he customarily did when he was concentrating intensely.

"It's dated five days ago," he announced at last, "and it's addressed to 'My dear Rafael.'"

"I believe that Señor Santora's given name is Rafael," said Mrs. Darnley. "He mentioned it the first time he came here. What else?"

"It's signed only with initials," said Jupiter. "A.F.G. I can't translate it exactly, but it goes something like this:

> My dear Rafael,
> I do not think you have made a mistake in telling Señora Darnley the history of the Chiavo glass, but it will take time to obtain the documents. If you can purchase the mirror without them, and very quickly, so much the better. I am very fearful of Juan Gómez. He is an evil man and can be dangerous. I am fearful for you and for Señora Darnley and also for the Republic of Ruffino. Gómez must not get the secret from the mirror. If he does, the bad days will never

end. I have learned that Juan Gómez has cousins in Los Angeles. They live in a place called Silverlake. Perhaps this is a help. Perhaps he stays with these cousins. If you can find where he stays, do so, and watch him. And try to get the glass. Above all, he must not have that mirror.

And for yourself, have great care. I feel I grow older. I am in a high place and I miss you and your support. It always makes me more refreshed when I see Ruffino through your eyes, which are younger and more keen than mine.

A.F.G.

Mrs. Darnley's face was thoughtful as Jupiter Jones finished his slow translation of the letter. "How very sad," she said. "That sounds like the letter from a lonely old man."

"A man in a high position," said Jupiter, "and a man who is afraid—afraid for Santora, for you, and for the Republic of Ruffino. Mrs. Darnley, I don't suppose you would know who wrote that letter? Does your friend, Señora Manolos, know a person with the initials A.F.G.? Her husband had a high position in Ruffino."

Mrs. Darnley shook her head. "Isabella Manolos and I have corresponded for years," she said, "ever since we were schoolgirls. But we only wrote about trifles. I couldn't bear that dreadful person she married, and I'm afraid she knew it."

"Grandma," said Jean, "when you don't like somebody, everybody knows it."

"Yes. Well, I suppose I sometimes say things I shouldn't. But I did not like Diego Manolos. I was never able to understand why Isabella married him, and after he began to get ahead and be important in that government job of his, I liked him even less. He had a horrid habit of smirking, as if he were smarter than anyone on earth. So I know very little about the government of Ruffino and the part Isabella's husband played in it. And no, I do not know who wrote that letter."

"Is there a world almanac in the house?" asked Bob. "The almanac always has lots of information on foreign countries."

Jean jumped up. "I bought one last year when I was doing crossword puzzles like crazy."

It took some searching among the books on the floor before the almanac turned up. Bob quickly checked the index at the back and flipped to the section on the Republic of Ruffino. It occupied only half a page in the book, and the information on the little island country was sparse.

"It's a democracy," Bob said as he skimmed through the paragraphs. "Sounds a lot like the United States government, except that it's much, much smaller. The lawmaking body is a senate plus a lower house with seventy-eight representatives. There is an executive council which advises the president . . ."

"Don't drag it out," complained Pete. "I can tell by the look on your face that you've found something."

Bob grinned. "There aren't any names given for the

senators or representatives, but the almanac gives the name of the president."

"Don't tell me!" said Pete. "Let me guess the initials."

"The president of the Republic of Ruffino is a man named Alfredo Felipe García," said Bob.

They sat quietly for a few moments. Then Jupiter got up and began to pace, pulling at his lip. "The president of the republic," he said. "That letter tells us a great deal, in spite of the fact that the man who wrote it tried to be so guarded. It tells us to beware of a man named Juan Gómez. I think we can assume that this Juan Gómez is our burglar, and that he and Santora are working against one another. Each one wants the glass. Today, Santora was injured by the burglar. I guess Gómez is indeed dangerous. Also, the letter tells us that Santora is not seeking the mirror for himself, but for someone high up in Ruffino. Something very important is at stake here, something to do with the goblin glass. I think we can safely conclude that Santora invented his connection to Chiavo. If he ever produces any documents from Spain they will undoubtedly be forgeries. For that matter, I doubt that Santora is Spanish. I think he is a citizen of Ruffino."

Mrs. Darnley shook her head. "Poor Isabella Manolos," she said. "If the person who wrote that letter is really the president of Ruffino, she may be in some difficulty. I think we should find out what it is before we stir up trouble and publicity."

"What do you mean, Grandma?" asked Jean.

"We really should call the police and report everything that has happened," said Mrs. Darnley. "However, perhaps that might be the worst thing we could possibly do." She looked at Jupiter, then at Bob and Pete. "I hired you to investigate my haunted looking glass," she said. "I hired you because Worthington has spoken well of you and also because I think young people sometimes *are* smarter than older ones. They don't have all those years of experience, so they don't have built-in expectations. They know that anything can happen."

"Quite so," put in Worthington.

"I understand, Mrs. Darnley," said Jupiter Jones. "I am sure we all know now that the haunted mirror is not haunted, but it must hold a secret. Shall we try to ascertain exactly what that secret is?"

Pete groaned. "It's late," he protested. "Also, I'm bushed, but . . . okay. Let's try. There must be something hidden somewhere, somehow."

Jeff went to the kitchen for a stepladder and tools. With mighty grunts and groans the four boys and Worthington managed to get the huge glass off the wall. Jupiter unscrewed the wooden backing from the steel frame. There was nothing underneath it. He went over every inch of the frame. There was nothing—nothing but the monstrous figures of those weird underworld creatures and the grotesque goblin at the top playing with the snake. There were no apertures in which anything could be hidden. There was only a huge, very ugly frame, an old mirror, and a wooden backing, which had been repaired several times. A number of smudged labels on the wood gave the names of craftsmen in Madrid and Ruffino who had worked on the glass.

Jupiter sat back on his heels and looked at the dismantled mirror. "And what in that could interest the president of a republic?"

10

The Magician's Cloak

Early the next morning Bob Andrews left Rocky Beach with his father. He was bound for Los Angeles, where he planned to go through back issues of the Los Angeles *Times* and look for stories about the Republic of Ruffino, and also about Drakestar the magician and his house in the Hollywood Hills.

Jupe and Pete caught a ride into Hollywood with Konrad, who had to deliver an old dining room table to a customer of The Jones Salvage Yard.

"Santora's still in the hospital," announced Jupe, as Konrad drove up the freeway. "I called hospitals in Beverly Hills last night until I located him. He's at the Beverly Crest Medical Center. Last night they weren't giving out any information and he wasn't taking calls. This morning I phoned again and they offered to put me through to his room, so he can't be badly hurt."

"I'm glad," said Pete. "I don't know whether he's a good guy or a bad guy, but I don't have to wonder about the man who hit him. I *know* he's a stinker."

"Juan Gómez," said Jupe. "The dangerous man named Juan Gómez. I went through the telephone directory this morning and found several people named Gómez in the Silverlake area. However, if Gómez *is* staying with a cousin there, we have no assurance that the cousin is also named Gómez or that he has a telephone. But let's not worry about him today."

"What *are* we going to do today?" asked Pete.

Jupe took a notebook out of his pocket. "I showed the piece of cloth that I tore from the phantom's robe to Aunt Mathilda," he said. "She agrees that it isn't an ordinary fabric. We'll call at the costume shops in Hollywood. Our ghost had to get that garment he wore somewhere, and what would be a more logical place than a costume shop?"

Pete scowled at Jupe's notebook. "I see you've made a list," he said. "How many costume shops are there?"

"Quite a few," admitted Jupe.

"My aching feet!" moaned Pete.

"Good detective work requires persistence," said Jupiter Jones sternly.

The truck turned off the freeway, and in a few minutes Konrad stopped at the corner of Sunset and Vine and the boys climbed out.

"You want me to pick you up later?" asked Konrad.

"No, we'll take the bus," said Jupiter. "We may be in Hollywood all day."

"Your Aunt Mathilda will be cross," warned Konrad. "She does not like it when you are away on Saturday."

"But she usually forgives us," said Jupe.

Konrad drove away and the boys began their search. The first costume shop on Jupiter's list was on Vine near Fountain. The Investigators went into a huge building, a place much like a warehouse. There was a small office area near the door where a jowly, balding man sat paging through a copy of a fashion magazine. Beyond the office the boys saw racks and racks of costumes of all sizes, colors, and descriptions.

The balding man looked up. "Yeah?" he said.

Jupiter took out the piece of fabric. "My aunt is trying to match this," he said. "She borrowed a costume for a party. She tore it and she has to get it fixed before she returns it. She hasn't been able to find the material in any of the regular shops. Do you have anything like it? Could you fix it?"

The man took the material and rubbed it between thumb and forefinger. "Hmm!" he said. "Wool. Dalton Mills used to make something like this, but we never used it." He handed the fabric back. "Sorry," he said.

The boys murmured their thanks and left.

"I feel like giving up right now," said Pete.

"We're only beginning," said Jupiter. "Places that

rent costumes never throw anything away. They mend and clean and keep things forever. It doesn't matter if the material isn't new.

At the second costume company the boys tried, the proprietor had never seen fabric like the piece Jupe showed him. It was the same at the third, fourth, and fifth shops the boys visited. It was almost eleven o'clock when Pete and Jupe came to a building on Santa Monica Boulevard which housed the Lancet Costume Company. Inside there was the usual office area, and there was a stout man leaning on a counter smoking a cigar.

Jupiter presented the piece of fabric and repeated the tale of the damaged costume. The man took the cigar out of his mouth and glared.

"Tell Baldini to do his own dirty work!" said the man.

"Baldini?" echoed Jupe.

"Don't act so dumb, kid," snapped the man. He picked up the piece of cloth. "Only one like this," he said, and his voice was suddenly a bit softer. "Dalton Mills used to make a wool that had silver threads, but it wasn't this good. This was woven for Drakestar the magician."

Jupe felt his heart give a thump.

"I was crazy to let that down-and-out Baldini rent Drakestar's robe," said the costume man. "Now you two get yourselves over to that crummy rooming house on Virginia and tell Baldini to bring back the robe. I can fix it, but it will cost him money. Can't do reweaving for nothing. Now beat it!"

"My aunt's fabric . . ." began Jupiter.

"Kid, that is not your aunt's fabric, and for all I know you don't have an aunt. Tell Baldini to bring the robe back or I may take five minutes off and go around and beat his ears down!"

Jupiter and Pete retreated with as much dignity as they could muster. When they were outside, Jupiter laughed out loud. "Wonderful! Someone named Baldini rents a robe which once belonged to Drakestar and then haunts a mirror in Drakestar's house! I was hoping we'd find the right costume shop and get a lead on the ghost, but this is too good! Our ghost is a real artist!"

"And he lives in a crummy rooming house on Virginia," said Pete. "It must be near here, if that man could go there in five minutes and beat his ears off."

"Shall we go?" said Jupiter Jones.

They went, excited now, and they found the rooming house easily. Most of the buildings on Virginia Avenue were fairly new apartment houses, but one old place which had once been a private residence remained. It was shabby, but the lawn was neatly mowed and there were flower beds near the porch. A sign in front indicated that a room was available.

"What now?" wondered Pete. "Do we walk up and ask for Baldini and see if he really is the ghost?"

"He might recognize me and that might not be a good idea," said Jupe. "Let's pretend we're doing a survey for . . . well, for our social studies class. We can talk to the landlady about how many people live in the house and what they do for a living."

"Fine," said Pete, "but you do it. You're better at that stuff than I am."

"Yes, I am" said Jupe. He took out his notebook, marched up the walk and rang the doorbell.

The door opened a crack and a gray-haired woman looked out. "Yes?" she said.

"I'm sorry to disturb you, ma'am," said Jupiter Jones. "We're doing a survey for a class at our school."

"But it's summer," said the woman. Her eyes suddenly narrowed with suspicion. "School's out."

Jupiter looked mournful. "Not for us, I'm afraid. We didn't pass the final exam in June and, well, we can make up the grade if we complete our project."

"It means an awful lot to us," said Pete.

"Well, all right." The door opened wider. "You look like nice boys. What do you want to know?"

"First," said Jupe, "how many people live here?"

"Six," she said. "Five boarders and myself."

Jupiter wrote this down.

"Are your tenants permanent residents?" asked Jupe. "Do they stay a long time or do they move often?"

"Oh, they stay!" The woman looked quite proud. "I make my guests comfortable, so they stay. Why, Mr. Henley has been here for five years."

"I see that you have a vacancy now." Jupe pointed toward the sign.

"Yes. Mr. Baldini moved out last night. Very sudden. Odd. But then people who've been in the theater can be odd, don't you think?"

"He'd been with you for a long time?"

"Four years," said the woman. "Funny, moving without any notice. He didn't even leave a change of address for the postman."

"That *is* strange," said Jupiter, "but then, as you say, people in the theater can be odd. Was he an actor?"

"Magician," said the woman. "That is, he used to be a magician. He doesn't get many bookings these days, so he sells newspapers. He has the stand on the corner of Santa Monica and Fountain."

"I see." Jupiter put the cap on his pen and closed his notebook. "Thank you very much. We only have to get four more interviews and we'll have the project finished. You've been very kind."

"Not at all," said the woman.

She closed the door and the boys hurried back to Santa Monica, where they boarded a bus.

"We have to make sure," said Jupe, "but I think, when we get to that newsstand at Fountain, Baldini will not be there."

Jupiter was right. The stand at the corner of Santa Monica and Fountain was shuttered and padlocked. Piles of papers bound with wire lay around on the sidewalk.

"He didn't even get in touch with his distributors," said Jupe. "Baldini, our phantom, has vanished!"

11
Disaster Strikes!

It was early afternoon when Jupiter Jones and Pete Crenshaw got off the bus in Rocky Beach.

"Let's not run into Aunt Mathilda," said Jupe. "She's not expecting us back so soon and if she sees us she's sure to put us to work. I want to call Bob and see what he's been able to find out at the *Times*."

"Red Gate Rover?" said Bob.

"Red Gate Rover," said Jupe.

The two circled around to the rear of The Jones Salvage Yard, where artists of Rocky Beach had decorated the junkyard fence with an exciting picture of the great San Francisco fire of 1906. At one place in the picture a little dog sat watching the flames. The dog's eye was a knothole. Jupe reached through this, undid a latch on the inside of the fence, then pushed on the boards. Three of them swung up. This was Red

Gate Rover. Jupe and Pete stepped through the opening to the inside of the salvage yard and made their
way along a narrow, hidden passageway between
walls of heaped-up junk to Headquarters.

There was no need to call Bob Andrews from the
telephone in Headquarters. The slender, bespectacled
boy was already in the office. He had magazines and
books spread out on the desk and was busy taking
notes.

Bob looked up when Jupe and Pete came into the
mobile home trailer through Door Four—a panel hidden from the outside by several heavy planks.

"You're back early," said Bob. "What did you find
out?"

Jupiter sat down on a straight chair across the desk
from Bob, and Pete pulled a chair in from the part of
the trailer which was devoted to laboratory work.

"We found out that the phantom of the looking
glass is almost certainly a vaudeville magician named
Baldini, and that he has disappeared."

"I'll bet Santora hired Baldini to perform and scare
Mrs. Darnley into giving up the glass," added Pete.

"You could be wrong," said Bob quietly.

"You found something?" asked Jupe. "Something
about Baldini?"

Bob nodded. "I made a note about it only because
the item mentioned Ruffino." He paged through his
papers. "I went through the microfilms of the *Times*
and I looked at everything I could find on Ruffino
and Drakestar. I knew that our ghost had to be famil-

iar with Drakestar's house, or he wouldn't have known about the secret room. Drakestar gave a lot of parties, and he liked to have newsmen present, so he did get mentioned in the papers. And one of his parties was for a newcomer—a stage magician who had just arrived in the United States from the island republic of Ruffino."

"How interesting," said Jupe.

"It is," Bob agreed. "Drakestar was officially retired, but he still performed for guests and he liked to give younger magicians a hand when he could. Baldini was one he tried to help. I guess Baldini never made the grade in this country, but that wasn't Drakestar's fault."

"So Baldini came from Ruffino," said Jupiter Jones. "The haunted mirror came from Ruffino, and someone in a high position in Ruffino wants the mirror and has sent Santora to try to get it. There is also our dangerous burglar, who is probably named Juan Gómez. Could Baldini have some reason of his own to want the mirror?"

"I think Santora hired him," said Pete stubbornly. "I think Santora is from Ruffino and he knew Baldini and hired him."

"Or Baldini could be trying to frighten Mrs. Darnley into selling the glass," mused Jupe. "Or perhaps he could be plotting with Gómez."

"If that Gómez wants the glass so much," said Bob, "and if he is plotting with Baldini, why didn't they just swipe it while no one was around? There are two of them and that house has been empty a couple of times this week."

"No. It's too heavy," Pete said. "It took the three of us and Jeff Parkinson and Worthington to get it off the wall. One or two men couldn't just walk out with it. But if Baldini was born in Ruffino he could still have friends there. He could know something about the glass. He could even know that Señora Manolos had it shipped to Mrs. Darnley."

"So he abandons his career as a newspaper vendor, rents Drakestar's old robe, and becomes the phantom who haunts the glass," said Jupe. "I like complicated puzzles, but we are beginning to have a few too many people involved in this one. So much for Baldini, at least for today. What did you find out about Ruffino?"

"I found four newspaper articles and one short book," said Bob. "Ruffino is a nice little island country where people grow sugar cane and bananas and the weather is pleasant and nothing much ever happens. It was a Spanish colony until 1872, when there was a revolution."

"Blood spilled all over, I suppose," said Pete.

"No. Everybody seems to have been pretty civilized about it," Bob said. "A group of influential merchants and politicians got together and told the governor from Spain that he wasn't welcome any more. They sent him home to Madrid. The Spanish didn't declare war, and the Ruffinians set up a government which runs a lot like ours does. The man who's presi-

dent now, Alfredo Felipe García, has been in office for two terms. According to a story in the back pages of the *Times* three months ago, he'll try for reelection again this winter. He'll be running against a former president—a guy named Simón de Pelar. He beat de Pelar twelve years ago."

"The presidential term of office is six years, then," said Jupiter.

"Yes, and there is no limit to the number of terms a president can serve. You can't believe everything you read in books, of course, but the history of Ruffino that I found gives de Pelar a very bad name. He loaded the public payrolls with his pals and he raised taxes. He had the police taking bribes from crooks, and García accused him of falsifying public records to get money. It was a pretty dirty campaign. De Pelar accused García of being a common thief in his youth. De Pelar swore he could prove it, only he couldn't. García won the election, and if you believe what's in the book, it was a darn good thing. If he hadn't won there might have been another revolution and it wouldn't have been bloodless."

Bob shoved the open book across the table toward Jupe and Pete. "There's a photograph of García with his advisers," he said.

Jupe took the book and examined the photograph. "García has the appearance of a trustworthy man," he decided, "not that appearances mean that much." He quickly read the caption and located the man called Diego Manolos, the late husband of Mrs.

Darnley's friend Isabella. Manolos was a tall man, very dark, with a slight squint. "Aunt Mathilda would say that his eyes were too close together," said Jupe.

"García's eyes?" said Bob, surprised.

"No. I was looking at Diego Manolos."

The telephone on the desk rang suddenly, stridently, startling The Three Investigators.

Bob picked it up. "Yes?" he said.

He listened. Then, "When?" he asked.

He listened again. "We'll be right there," he promised.

"What is it?" asked Jupiter Jones, after Bob hung up.

"Jean Parkinson," said Bob. "Jeff left the house this morning to go to a hobby shop in Hollywood. He didn't come back. Instead, a note was just shoved through the letter slot. Jeff's been kidnapped! Jean wants us to come right away. She couldn't reach Worthington, so we're to take a cab!"

12
Where Is Jeff?

It was barely three when the cab driver delivered The Three Investigators to the Darnley house. The boys went inside to find Mrs. Darnley pacing in the big living room. Jean crouched in a chair, pulling at a lock of hair, and glowering at the mirrors in which her grandmother's ceaseless movement was repeated again and again.

"Mrs. Darnley, have you called the police?" said Jupiter.

"No, and I'm not going to. The kidnapper warned me not to."

"Kidnapping is a very serious crime," Jupiter pointed out. "And the police are always careful not to do anything to endanger the victim."

"They are not going to have a chance to endanger Jeff!" she cried. She handed him an opened envelope.

Jupe took out the single piece of paper which it contained. He looked it over quickly, then read it aloud:

Mrs. Darnley, I have your grandson. Do not doubt it and do not summon the police. He himself will make the telephone call to you. He will call today and tell you what you must do to make him again free. I hope you will do what he says. I can be cruel, but when I am it always is for good reason.

Jupe turned the note over in his hands. "Cheap paper," he said. "You can get this in any dime store. Block printing. The kidnapper used a ball-point pen. And I would say the letter was not written by an American. And I can guess what the ransom will be."

"We can all guess," said Jean. "The goblin glass."

"They can have it!" cried Mrs. Darnley. "I'm sorry I ever laid eyes on the horrible thing! If that beast Santora has . . ."

"Señor Santora is in the hospital," said Bob. "Uh . . . that is, he was in the hospital this morning."

Jupiter Jones suddenly jumped up. "Good night!" he exclaimed. "Yes, he *was* in the hospital, but he could have been released. We'd better find out."

In seconds, Jupe was on the telephone, dialing the number of the Beverly Crest Medical Center. He spoke briefly to the hospital operator, then said, "I see. Thank you," and hung up.

"Santora has been discharged," he said. "What time did Jeff leave for the hobby shop?"

"Eleven," said Jean. "Maybe eleven thirty."

"Then the kidnapper could be Santora," decided Jupe. "Even if he was discharged as late as ten thirty he could have done it."

Jupe made another call then to the Beverly Sunset Hotel. The hotel operator put him through to Santora's room, and Santora answered. Jupe quickly hung up.

"So Santora's at his hotel," said Bob. "Want me to go over and keep an eye on him? Somebody might remember seeing Pete there yesterday."

Mrs. Darnley took her pocketbook from the coffee table, pulled several bills from a change purse, and gave them to Bob. "Call a cab," she ordered. "And call here when you get to the hotel."

He took the money. "I will. And I won't let Santora see me, so don't worry."

Bob left and the four people in the living room sat in gloomy silence, Jupiter frowning, Pete going from mirror to mirror, looking into the glasses as if he had never seen his own face before.

At quarter to four the telephone rang. Jean jumped and so did Jupiter. Mrs. Darnley strode to the desk where the telephone stood and picked it up. "What do you want?" she said. Her voice was rough.

After a second she said, "Oh, thanks," and put down the telephone.

"Was that Bob?" asked Jupiter Jones.

"Yes. He said Santora was having a late lunch in the coffee shop. Bob is in the hotel lobby and he'll stay there."

"So much for that, for the moment," said Jupiter Jones.

"I wish we knew where that burglar is right now," said Pete. "Also Baldini."

"Baldini?" echoed Jean. "Who's he?"

"A magician from Ruffino," Jupiter told her, "and your former ghost."

"Oh, good heavens!" exclaimed Mrs. Darnley. "Another character from that awful place! I wish I'd never heard of it. I wish I'd never met Isabella Manolos."

The telephone rang again.

"That must be it!" said Mrs. Darnley. Suddenly she began to tremble.

There was another ring.

"You answer," said Jupiter. "I'll listen on the extension in the kitchen."

He sped out of the room and down the hall to the kitchen, where John Chan was stolidly polishing silver. Carefully he lifted the receiver from the extension near the stove.

"I'm okay, Grandma," Jupe heard Jeff say.

"Thank heavens!"

"I can't say where I am," said Jeff. "I have to just tell you what to do and then hang up, okay?"

"Okay. Tell me and I'll do it."

"There's a warehouse in San Pedro," said Jeff. "It's on Ocean Boulevard, and there's a sign out in front that says it's The Peckham Storage Company—only it's empty."

"An abandoned warehouse, Ocean Boulevard, San Pedro," repeated Mrs. Darnley. "I'm writing it down."

"You're to have the Chiavo glass delivered there," said Jeff. "Call a moving company or a trucker or somebody and have them take the mirror and leave it in the warehouse and then go away. They've got to lean it against a post toward the back end of the warehouse and just go away. And Grandma?"

"What, Jeff?"

"It has to be there by seven tonight."

"It will be," said Mrs. Darnley.

"I'll call you after," said Jeff. "He said I can call you again, but not until he has the mirror."

With that, the telephone clicked and the line went dead.

13

The Telltale Bells

"Where can I get a trucker at this hour?" moaned Mrs. Darnley. "It's after four! Suppose I can't get a trucker?"

"I'll call my uncle," said Jupiter. "He can come with Hans and Konrad. He'll be glad to do it, Mrs. Darnley. Don't worry. The mirror will be in San Pedro by seven."

"Oh, thank you, Jupiter." She sat down on the sofa. "Would you mind calling your uncle right away? It'll take time to get that mirror down and we don't want to be late."

Jupe went to the telephone, lifted the receiver, then paused, stared at the wall for a second, and quietly replaced the receiver.

"Jupiter, we don't have much time!" cried Mrs. Darnley. "Do hurry up and call your uncle."

"Just a second," said Jupe. "There was something on the telephone when Jeff made his call. Something in the background. Music. Did you hear it?"

"Music?" Mrs. Darnley looked bewildered. "I . . . I only heard Jeff. But what if there was music? It doesn't mean anything. Jupiter, make the call."

"Chimes," said Jupe. "There were chimes playing a little tune. I didn't hear them at first. Then I heard them quite loudly, and then they faded away again. They were playing 'Mary Had a Little Lamb.' "

"The ice cream man," said Pete. He stopped his wandering from mirror to mirror and stood on the hearth. "The Meadow Fresh Ice Cream people have trucks that drive around and play chimes. They play 'Mary Had a Little Lamb.' "

Jupe sat down next to the desk. "It could be a clue," he said. "It could tell us where Jeff is being held. I think we can take it for granted that he's *not* in San Pedro, or at least that he's not in that deserted warehouse. The kidnapper wouldn't risk holding him there. It was almost exactly four o'clock when Jeff made that telephone call. At about four, a Meadow Fresh Ice Cream truck passed the place where Jeff is a prisoner, and then there was something else." Jupe closed his eyes and concentrated, trying to remember every detail of the telephone call. "A clanging," he said. "After the ice cream truck passed, there was another ringing noise. But it was loud—like a burglar alarm. And then there was a kind of vibration."

"You've got the most astonishing memory," exclaimed Mrs. Darnley. "All I heard was Jeff talking."

"Total recall," Pete told her. "Jupe's famous for it. He never forgets anything."

"An ice cream truck," said Jupe, "and a clanging sound and then a vibration. A railroad crossing! That's what happens at a railroad crossing! There's a warning signal, flashing lights, and a bell that rings to alert drivers that a train is coming. Then the rumble would be the train going by. Wherever Jeff is, an ice cream truck went by there at four, and it's very near a railroad crossing where a train went by a second or two later."

"There must be dozens of those ice cream trucks in Los Angeles," said Jean.

"But there aren't dozens of railroad crossings," said Jupe, "and those trucks have regular routes. The ice cream man comes to Rocky Beach at about three every afternoon. He's never more than twenty minutes off. If we can get to the Meadow Fresh people . . ."

"But what if it wasn't a train?" said Mrs. Darnley. "It could be a place where a burglar alarm went off—they do go off sometimes, you know—and then a truck went by."

"No," said Jupiter Jones. "A truck would take only a second to pass any given spot. This rumbling sound continued for some time. It has to be a train. With any luck at all, we could get to Jeff before the glass is delivered to the kidnapper."

"You can try," said Mrs. Darnley, "but I refuse to

let you take chances with my grandson's life. Please, call your uncle and have him come with the truck."

"Of course." Jupiter picked up the telephone, dialed the number of The Jones Salvage Yard, and heard his Aunt Mathilda answer at the other end.

"Jupiter Jones, where are you?" said Aunt Mathilda. "What have you been doing? You've been gone all day and Konrad said . . ."

"I'm sorry, Aunt Mathilda," said Jupiter quickly. "I can't explain now. I'll tell you about it later. Is Uncle Titus there?"

Aunt Mathilda said nothing for a moment, and Jupe could picture her frowning and irritated, but then she called Uncle Titus to the telephone.

"I'm with Mrs. Darnley," Jupe told his uncle. "She's in great trouble and she needs help. Could you bring one of the trucks here right away? And bring Hans and Konrad with you. That big looking glass in Mrs. Darnley's library has to be delivered to a warehouse in San Pedro before seven o'clock tonight, and it's heavy. You'll need help."

"Jupiter, are you on one of your cases?" asked Uncle Titus.

"Yes, and I don't have time . . ."

"It's all right," said Uncle Titus quickly. "I'll come."

Jupe grinned, thanked his uncle, and hung up. "You can be sure the glass will be delivered," he told Mrs. Darnley.

Pete had taken a Los Angeles telephone directory

from the bottom shelf of a bookcase. "The Meadow Fresh main office is on Macy Street," he said, "down near the Union Depot. That area's got more railroad tracks than anything this side of Chicago. Could Jeff be down there someplace?"

Jupe shook his head. "Unlikely. The Meadow Fresh people keep their trucks on the streets until quite late in the summer. At four in the afternoon the trucks wouldn't be anywhere near the main office. They'd be out in the neighborhoods where there are children. But there has to be a dispatcher—someone we can talk to who knows the routes."

"You'd better go to the office in person," said Mrs. Darnley. "You'll never get that sort of information by telephone. Here." She took some more bills from her pocketbook and gave them to Jupe. "Go find out what you can from the ice cream people. I'll stay here and wait for your uncle and see that the mirror gets on its way. And be careful. I don't care about the goblin glass. I only want Jeff back, and I want him safe and sound."

"I'll be very careful," promised Jupe.

"I'll go with Jupe, in case we have to split up," said Pete.

Mrs. Darnley nodded.

"I'm going, too," announced Jean Parkinson.

"You are not," said her grandmother. "I will not have both my grandchildren endangered. You will not leave this house until Jeff is back!"

14

To the Rescue!

The Meadow Fresh Ice Cream Company was a long, low building surrounded by sun-parched macadam. There was not an ice cream truck in sight when the taxi crossed the parking lot toward the loading platform of the ice cream plant.

"Don't know what you kids want here," said the cab driver. "They don't sell any ice cream out of here. You've got to buy it from one of those trucks."

"We're making arrangements for a party," said Jupiter Jones.

The driver pulled up next to the loading platform. Jupiter took out the money Mrs. Darnley had given him and handed a ten dollar bill to the driver. "Hold this and wait for us," he ordered.

Jupe and Bob climbed onto the loading dock, opened one of a pair of double doors, and stepped

into an office that was empty except for an elderly
man with thick glasses. He sat with a telephone at his
ear and made notes on a huge, ruled sheet of paper
spread out before him.

"Okay, Flannery," he said into the telephone.
"You're running a little late but that's okay. Don't try
to get past the stadium until after eight. There's a
night game. No sense in getting hung up in that
traffic."

He put down the telephone, took off the thick
glasses, and peered at the Investigators. "Yes?" he
said.

Jupiter Jones pointed to an oversized street map of
greater Los Angeles hanging on the wall behind the
man. The map was in black and white, with stripes of
red, blue, green, orange, yellow, purple, and brown
radiating out from the area of Macy Street to the far
reaches of the city.

"I assume," said Jupiter, "that the markings on that
map indicate the routes taken by your ice cream
trucks."

"You assume correctly," said the man. "What
about it?"

"Your drivers call in to you from various points
along their routes?" asked Jupiter.

"You bet they do," said the man. "We like to keep
track of our guys. We don't hear from them, we call
the cops. There've been a couple of holdups. What's it
to you?"

"It's essential that we locate any driver who passed

a railroad crossing where there is a warning bell that rang at four this afternoon."

The telephone on the desk rang.

"Please," said Jupiter. His voice was soft, but very serious. "Don't answer that. Let it ring for a minute. It's very important."

The man picked up the telephone. "Meadow Fresh," he said. Then, "Okay, Guilberti, hold it a second, will you? I've got a couple of medium-sized problems here."

He put the telephone down on the desk. "Make it snappy," he said. "What's up, anyhow? You get short-changed by one of our men?"

"I haven't time to explain," said Jupiter Jones. "If you can just tell us which of your drivers would have been at a railroad right-of-way at about four . . ."

"It could save someone's life," Pete suddenly put in.

The man stared. Then, impressed by the serious looks on the boys' faces, he ran his finger down a series of entries on the sheet in front of him.

"Alberts crosses the Santa Fé tracks at LaBrea," he said, "but he went by there before three. Couldn't be him. No. Let's see. Yeah. Yeah, it must have been Charlie Swanson. His route takes him out past that grade crossing on Hamilton." The man stood up and pointed to a spot on the big map. It was in the San Fernando Valley. "He called me from a gas station near there at ten after four, so he'd have been southbound on Hamilton at about four. Do you want to get in touch with him?"

"Not necessarily," said Jupiter Jones. "Thank you very much."

The boys ran from the office, tumbled down from the loading platform, and yanked open the cab door.

"Quick!" said Jupiter to the driver, and gave him the directions. "It's an emergency!"

"Whatever you say," answered the driver with a shrug. He did his best to hurry, threading his way through the downtown traffic and then out along the Hollywood Freeway to the San Fernando Valley. Luckily for the Investigators, traffic was moving steadily. In thirty minutes, the cab was proceeding north on Hamilton.

"Now drive very slowly," ordered Jupe, and he and Pete carefully surveyed each side of the street. At first it was lined with small homes, and then there were only vacant lots. Realtors' signs could be seen here and there announcing that the land was for sale. They saw the grade crossing ahead. It was guarded by an automatic signal, now silent. The driver slowed at the crossing and glanced up and down the tracks. Jupe saw that on the far side of the tracks there was a single house—a dingy, weather-stained bungalow which might once have been part of a citrus ranch. A few lemon trees, looking forlorn and neglected, still stood in back of the place. The house itself was decayed, with rusted screens torn from the windows in several places, and several boards missing from the front porch.

"Well?" said the cabbie.

"Keep driving," ordered Jupiter.

They went on past more open lots and more real estate signs. After another block they again saw small homes, neatly kept lawns, and children playing on the sidewalks in the late afternoon sun.

"Turn right at the next corner," Jupiter instructed.

The cabbie complied. He parked at the curb in front of a house where a man was watering the lawn.

"Well?" said the cabbie again. "Where to now?"

"Let me think," said Jupiter. "It must be that old house near the railroad tracks. The other places aren't near enough to that warning signal. I heard it very clearly when Jeff made his telephone call."

"Yes," agreed Pete. "It's the only place. And what a spot to hide someone. Even if he yelled nobody'd hear it."

The driver cleared his throat. "Did we come way out here to look at a run-down old farmhouse?"

"How do we get in there?" said Jupe.

"Why do you want to?" asked the driver. "You can tell nobody lives there, but if you . . ."

"Somebody *is* in there," said Jupe, "and we have to get in without being seen. I think I know how."

He had spotted a small bakery truck coming down the street. It stopped about fifty yards from them, and its horn sounded a series of cheery notes. The driver climbed out with a basket of bread and other baked things when a young woman came out of one of the houses. She selected several packages from the basket and handed the bakery man some money.

"That's it!" cried Jupe. "We'll deliver some bread!"

"Great!" cried Pete. He jumped out of the cab and ran toward the bakery truck, waving his arms.

"You kids are nuts," said the cabbie as Jupe started after Pete. "You want me to wait? You already have fifteen dollars on the meter and . . ."

Jupe handed him another ten dollar bill. "Keep the change," he said, "and if you see us get aboard that bread truck, don't wait. We won't need you."

"Suits me," said the cabbie.

Jupe came up to the bread man, a thin, sunburned young fellow who might have been in his late teens or early twenties. "But I'm not allowed to pick up riders," he was saying.

"We don't want a ride, exactly," said Pete. "We want to make a delivery at a house near here."

The cab pulled up near the bread truck and the driver leaned out. "Everything okay?" asked the cabbie.

"No, it's not okay," said the young bread man. "This is my first job. I don't want to goof it."

"I know," said Jupe earnestly. "We won't make any trouble, honestly. Look, what's your name?"

"Henry. Henry Anderson."

"Well, look, Mr. Anderson . . ."

"Just call me Henry. But *you* look—if I blow this chance, I'm back in the line at the unemployment office."

Jupiter nodded. "We represent Mrs. Jonathan

Darnley," he said. He took out his wallet and handed one of the cards of The Three Investigators to the young man. "We have reason to believe that Mrs. Darnley's grandson is being held prisoner in that house."

"Mrs. Darnley?" said Henry Anderson. "I've seen her picture in the papers. But . . . The Three Investigators? I never heard of The Three Investigators."

"I am Jupiter Jones," said Jupe, "and this is Pete Crenshaw. Our partner, Bob Andrews, is keeping a suspect under surveillance in Beverly Hills."

"Like a television show, isn't it?" said the cab driver.

"And we *are* detectives," Jupiter assured the bread man. "We have succeeded in solving mysteries in many cases where the police have failed. In this case, the police haven't been called in. Mrs. Darnley is afraid that the kidnapper will harm her grandson."

Henry Anderson turned the card over as if he might find a magical solution to his dilemma printed on the back. He looked at Jupe, then at Pete.

"We ought to hurry," said Pete. A horrible thought had come to him. "We think Jeff is okay, but we don't know for sure. He was okay at four this afternoon, when he telephoned his grandmother about the ransom."

"The police . . ." said Henry Anderson helplessly.

"We don't dare," said Jupe. "Mrs. Darnley won't hear of it. We have to get Jeff back ourselves."

"Okay," said Henry Anderson. "Okay, okay, okay!

I'm probably as nutty as you are, but if you're telling the truth and I don't help . . ."

"Lots of luck," said the cab driver. He drove off.

"What do you want me to do?" asked Anderson.

"Lend me your cap and your jacket," said Jupe. "Then drive down Hamilton past the old house near the railroad tracks. Stop there, and I'll get out and go up and ring the doorbell."

"I don't usually ring doorbells," said Anderson. "I just blow my horn and people come out."

"If the kidnapper is the one we think he is, he won't know that," Jupiter assured him.

Two minutes later the bread truck was making its way down Hamilton, past the empty lots and the real estate signs. In the back Jupe was putting on Henry Anderson's jacket and cap. Pete crouched on the floor, steadying himself by leaning against trays of rolls and bread and cupcakes and cookies.

"Watch it, huh?" said Pete to Jupiter.

"Don't worry," Jupe assured him. "If I go in and don't come out again . . ."

"It'll mean we don't have much to lose, won't it?" said Pete. "If that happens, I'll come after you."

"Me, too," volunteered Henry Anderson. He stopped in front of the dilapidated farmhouse. "This it?"

"Right." Jupe climbed down. The jacket was open, since he was a shade too plump to get it buttoned. He took the basket of baked things, began to whistle, and walked up a broken strip of concrete to the steps of

the tumble-down house. He mounted carefully to the porch, testing each board before he put his weight on it. There was no doorbell, so he knocked loudly.

He waited. No one moved inside the old house.

He knocked again. "Van Alstyn's Bakery!" he cried. "Anybody home?"

Still there was silence inside the house. Jupe took a step to the right and peeked through a front window. He saw emptiness, dust, and stains where rain had come through the walls. He also saw something that made his heart beat faster. There was a clear path through the dust on the floor of the front room. Something had been dragged from that room out toward the back of the house. And in one corner of that dirty, empty place, there was a telephone—a new, modern, sparkling white telephone!

Jupe put the bakery basket down on the porch and tried to turn the doorknob. It was locked, but the window next to the door was unlatched. Jupe got his fingers under the sash and pulled.

The window came open with a loud screech.

Still no one moved inside the house.

Jupe put a leg over the window sill and climbed into the place. Beyond the front room with its torn wallpaper, there was a kitchen. Jupe could see worn linoleum and an old sink. He went swiftly to the kitchen door. Then he stopped.

Jeff Parkinson was there! He was on the floor, very securely tied up. A soiled handkerchief hid his mouth, but his eyes were open and alert. When he saw Jupe his eyes crinkled a bit, as if he were trying to smile.

15

A Race Against Time

Jeff sat in the middle of the kitchen and rubbed his ankles with both hands. "My feet are numb," he complained. He grinned at Jupe, and at Pete and Henry Anderson, who had come running from the bread truck when Jupe called. "Am I ever glad to see you guys," said Jeff. "I wasn't sure that little crook was going to come back here and let me go, once he had the looking glass. After I called my grandmother he dragged me out here to the kitchen in case anybody got curious about his car being parked out front and started peeking in the windows."

"Little crook?" said Jupiter. "That eliminates Señor Santora and also the phantom of the mirror. Neither of them are small. I assume you mean the burglar."

"It was him, and his name *is* Juan Gómez. He didn't bother to tell me why he wants the mirror."

"You'd better call Mrs. Darnley," advised Pete.

Jeff nodded, got up, and made his way unsteadily to the white telephone in the living room. He sat down beside it and dialed the number of the Darnley house. The three listeners in the old house in the valley heard the sound of a single ring at the other end, and then Jeff was saying, "Hello, Grandma. It's me, Jeff. I'm okay."

Incoherent sounds came through the receiver. "I'm *really* okay," said Jeff. "Jupe and Pete found me."

Jeff talked another minute and then handed the phone to Jupe. "She's putting Bob on," he said.

"Bob? I thought Bob was in Beverly Hills, watching Santora!" Jupe took the telephone. "Bob? What happened?" he asked. "Where's Santora?"

"I blew it!" said Bob. He sounded very discouraged. "He got away from me. About four he came down from his room and went out. I went after him. He had a car parked on a side street down from the hotel. He got into it and drove off, and there wasn't a cab in sight. I called Mrs. Darnley, and Jean said you were out trying to find Jeff, so I came back here."

"What about the mirror?" Jupiter asked.

"Your uncle and Hans and Konrad left a couple of minutes ago for San Pedro," Bob told him. "They've got the glass loaded on the truck and they're going to deliver it, as requested. Say, where are you, anyway? Is Jeff really okay? Mrs. Darnley wants . . ."

Bob broke off in midsentence, and Jupe heard Mrs. Darnley's voice.

"Who kidnapped my grandson?" she demanded.

"The small man who broke into your house and was found in the library, Mrs. Darnley," said Jupe.

"Juan Gómez?" said Mrs. Darnley.

"That's his name," said Jupiter. "Jeff tells me that he is now on his way to San Pedro."

"I didn't get the license number of his car," groaned Jeff. "Oh, blast! I didn't get the number. I was too scared. He had a gun."

"Never mind," said Jupiter Jones. "Mrs. Darnley, since Jeff is out of danger, you can call the police and have that warehouse in San Pedro surrounded. Uncle Titus and Hans and Konrad will deliver the mirror, and when Gómez shows up to get it the police can arrest him. Then you'll have the kidnapper only . . ." Jupe paused and grinned, "only, if you do that, we may never find out exactly how the puzzle fits together. We may never know how he's connected to Santora, or to Baldini, that magician who impersonated the ghost of Chiavo."

"I intend to know everything," said Mrs. Darnley.

"Good!" said Jupiter Jones. "Then we don't have any time to waste. Pete and I will go straight to that warehouse. Tell Bob to meet us in San Pedro. Tell him to stand where he can see us when we come off the freeway. We'll be in a cab and we'll stop at the intersection and . . ."

"You won't be in a cab!" protested Henry Anderson suddenly.

"What?" said Jupiter Jones.

"I said, you won't be in a cab. You'll be in a bread truck! I took a chance on you guys, and you were telling me the truth. So I want to be in on this all the way."

"A bread truck!" cried Pete. "Beautiful! Who'd ever suspect a bread man of being a detective!"

"We'll be in a truck belonging to the Van Alstyn Bakery Company," Jupiter said into the telephone. "We'll pick up Bob and watch for the kidnapper go into the warehouse. If he has a confederate we might see him too. That glass is too heavy for one man. He must have a confederate!"

Jeff took the telephone. "Grandma, I'm going with Jupe and Pete." He hung up before she could protest.

"Let's go!" said Pete. "It's almost six!"

"Ocean Avenue?" said Henry Anderson, the bread man. "You said San Pedro. That where we're going?"

"That's it," Pete told him. "And we've got to get there before seven. Think we can make it?"

Anderson grinned. "We may mash a couple of cupcakes on the way, but we'll make it," he promised.

The Investigators, Jeff, and Anderson hurried out to the truck. Pete and Jeff got into the back, sat on the floor, and braced themselves against the trays of baked goods. Jupiter sat on the floor in front, next to the single seat provided for the driver. Henry Anderson slammed the door shut, gunned his engine as if he were at the starting line in an auto race, and they were off. It took Anderson only ten minutes to get to the Hollywood Freeway, where he immediately pushed his truck up to the legal limit.

"Can't we go any faster?" cried Pete from the rear. "It's five after six!"

"If I go over the speed limit or change lanes too much the Highway Patrol will pull us over," Anderson yelled back. "Take it easy. We'll make it!"

It was only six twenty-five when the truck turned off onto the Harbor Freeway toward the warehouse in San Pedro. Almost immediately, Anderson had to slow down.

"What is it?" demanded Pete.

"Traffic, is all," said Anderson. "It's okay. It's moving. Lucky it's Saturday or we could be jammed in here solid."

Pete sweated and fumed in the back. Henry Anderson kept assuring him that all would be well, but Jupe noticed that Anderson was beginning to be a bit worried.

Then traffic thinned out and the truck picked up speed again. It raced along the fast lane, next to the center divider of the freeway. As they neared the coast, the late sunlight faded.

"We'll hit fog," said Anderson. "The harbor's going to be fogged in."

"We'll manage," Jupe assured him. "We've worked in fog before."

"We're almost there." Anderson eased his truck over and went down the ramp onto Ocean Avenue.

At the first intersection on Ocean, Anderson stopped the truck. "Want me to blow my horn?"

"No. Bob started from Hollywood, so he had a good lead on us. He's here somewhere. Let him find us."

"It's ten minutes of seven!" yelled Pete.

"Which means we have ten whole minutes," Jupe replied.

A slim figure darted out of a doorway across the street. "That your friend?" asked Anderson, pointing. Jupe stood up. "It's Bob." He waved. Bob waved back, then raced across the street and climbed into the truck.

"Sorry I lost Santora," he said, and he smiled back at Jeff Parkinson. "You scared the fool out of everybody."

"Especially me," said Jeff. "I have never been so scared in my entire life!"

"We can talk about it later," said Jupiter Jones sharply. "Drive on down Ocean," he told Anderson. "Drive slowly, as if you were waiting for someone to come out and buy bread from you."

Anderson did as he was told. "Actually, we do have a truck that covers the San Pedro area," he told the boys. "The driver works an early shift. He sells a lot of stuff to the men who work on the docks and in the trucking places around here. What are we looking for?"

"An abandoned warehouse which used to be run by a firm called the Peckham Storage Company. There will be a sign out in front with the name of the firm. When we get to it, can you pretend the truck is stalled and you can't get it started again?"

"Easy," said Anderson.

They cruised along a boulevard that was almost entirely deserted. The warehouses and shipping offices on either side of the street had closed for the day. A car passed them going west toward the freeway, and on the sidewalk a man in coveralls trudged along carrying a jacket. As they neared Ocean Boulevard fog was beginning to drift in between the buildings. They passed piers which seemed lifeless, and beyond the piers they glimpsed the harbor.

"There it is," said Anderson softly.

Jupe and Bob got to their knees and looked out through the windshield. On their right was a square brick building, much grimed with age and soot. The sign in front was faded but still readable. The larger of the two trucks owned by Uncle Titus stood in front of the warehouse.

"Uncle Titus and Hans and Konrad are still here," Jupe informed his friends in the back of the truck.

"That means the kidnapper isn't, just yet," said Pete. There was great relief in his voice.

"Pull up past that truck," Jupe ordered Anderson. "Go on for half a block, and then stop your engine."

The bread man went slowly past the warehouse, then let the truck swerve toward the curb and turned off the ignition.

Jupe and Bob scrambled toward the back of the truck and looked out the rear window. They saw Uncle Titus come out of the warehouse and climb into the cab of the salvage yard truck. Hans and Konrad followed him.

"All right," said Jupe. "The instructions have been followed to the letter. Now all we have to do is wait."

Henry Anderson began to get out of the truck.

"Where are you going?" asked Pete.

"I've got to tinker with the motor," said Anderson. "What's the first thing a guy does when his truck stalls? He gets out and tinkers with the motor. Wouldn't look natural if he didn't."

Jupiter Jones chuckled. "You have the makings of a first-rate detective, Henry Anderson!"

16
The Fight
for the Haunted Glass

Henry Anderson poked and pried at the motor of the bread truck. He unscrewed spark plugs, wiped them off and replaced them, looked into the radiator, and examined the battery.

In the truck The Three Investigators and Jeff Parkinson crouched low. Jupe peeped out of the windshield, keeping his head down so that no one on the street would see him. Pete, on his knees, surveyed the street through the rear window of the truck.

"I don't like it," said Pete, finally. "The fog's getting thicker, and it's beginning to get dark. That crook could already be inside the warehouse, and if he stays there long, we'll miss him when he comes out."

"I don't think he's inside," said Jupiter Jones. "He'd be foolish to wait inside for the mirror to be delivered. If Mrs. Darnley had called the police he'd be trapped in there. My guess is that he's cruising around, checking to make sure the police *aren't* waiting for him. If he is, perhaps he's suspicious of our friend Henry."

Jupe rapped softly on the inside of the windshield. Henry Anderson came around to the side of the truck.

"Maybe you'd better stop fooling with the motor," said Jupe. "Why not pretend you're going to telephone for help? Isn't that what you'd do if you were really stuck?"

Anderson nodded.

"Good. Go and locate a telephone. We'll need one, anyway, if the kidnapper shows up. Then come back here. We think you may be making our kidnapper nervous."

"Wouldn't want to do that," said Anderson, and he started off down the street. Five minutes passed, then—

"Look!" said Pete.

Jupe scrambled to the back of the truck. Pete pointed. A thin, black-clad man had stepped out from the far side of a fence that surrounded a lumberyard. He stood looking suspiciously at the bread truck.

"That *is* him, isn't it?" Jupe asked Jeff Parkinson.

"I think so," said Jeff. "Hard to tell in this fog."

"We'll know in a minute," said Bob.

The man started along the sidewalk toward the truck.

"Geehosephat!" breathed Pete. "He's headed this way!"

"It *is* Gómez!" added Jeff. "What do we do now?"

"Get down! Quick!" snapped Jupiter.

Just then the cheery voice of Henry Anderson sounded outside the truck.

"Evening," said Anderson.

"Yes," said the kidnapper. "You work late today, I think."

"Trying to pick up a few extra bucks," said Anderson. "Rotten idea. Didn't know San Pedro was so empty on a Saturday night—and now my truck's broken down. I'm in hot water with my boss. Say, I don't suppose I could interest you in a loaf of bread or anything?"

"A loaf of bread? Yes. Yes, I think that would be very nice. I would like to see your bread."

The boys crouched in the very rear of the truck and tried to make themselves as small as possible. Henry Anderson clambered into the cab and groped for his basket of baked goods.

Bob seized the bakery basket and thrust it at Henry. Henry turned, almost bumping the kidnapper with it. "I've got plain white bread," said Henry, "rye, whole wheat, pumpernickel, sour dough French bread, and . . ."

The man sniffed. "I think," he said, "that I do not wish any bread after all."

"French pastry?" asked Henry. "Cupcakes?"

"Nothing, I thank you. Sorry to trouble you."

"No trouble," said Henry. "I've got to wait for the tow truck anyway."

"Then I wish you a good evening," said the man. "Thanks."

The man turned back toward the warehouse.

The Three Investigators breathed more easily. "That was close," said Bob. "You got here just in time, Henry."

"There's a telephone booth at the service station two blocks east," reported Henry.

The Investigators watched the kidnapper cross the street, go up to the door of the warehouse, and after one quick glance over his shoulder, pull open the door and go into the place.

"Do we go in after him?" asked Jeff.

"Let's wait a bit," said Jupiter quietly.

Then there was another figure on the street—a taller man had appeared from behind the fence that protected the lumberyard. This second person did not glance to left or to right. He went directly to the door of the warehouse and entered the place.

"I think that was Santora," said Pete.

"Exactly what I hoped would happen!" exclaimed Jupiter Jones. "Now we will invade that place and see what's to be seen and hear what's to be heard. Henry, give us ten minutes in there, and then go to that telephone booth and call the police. Whatever happens, we're going to need them."

"Right," said Henry.

The Investigators and Jeff Parkinson climbed out

of the bread truck and went quickly to the warehouse. They paused at the door.

"Can't hear anything," Bob whispered. "Nothing but water sloshing. This place must be built out over the harbor."

He pulled on the door handle. The door opened silently and the boys saw walls and another door. There was a barred window high up and to the right, and this let in the fading, fog-filled evening light. They were in a small, empty room facing a pair of double doors with glass set into the upper panels.

They crept to the inner doors, looked through dirty panes, and saw a huge open area. There were skylights in the high ceiling and deep shadows in the corners. At the far end of the place Juan Gómez stood looking at the goblin glass. Uncle Titus and his helpers had stood the mirror upright, leaning it against one of the steel beams that supported the roof.

Between the kidnapper and the boys, there was the silhouetted figure of Santora. The mystery man who claimed to be the descendant of the magician Chiavo was motionless, watching even as the boys were watching. Jupe pressed on one of the doors and it opened a crack. He and the others stood, trying not to breathe, and they watched and listened.

The kidnapper ran his fingers carefully over the frame of the mirror. Then he walked slowly around the glass, finally pulling a screwdriver out of his pocket.

"What are you looking for, you servant of a pig?"

said Santora suddenly.

The kidnapper started, dropped his screwdriver, and stared at Santora in the dim light.

"Do not move," said Santora. "I have a gun, and I would not fear to use it."

Santora walked forward, and the boys saw that he did indeed have a gun. It was pointed directly at the kidnapper's head.

"Gómez, would you carry this infamy on forever?" demanded Santora. "Manolos is dead and his widow lives in peace. She knows nothing."

"She is a fool," said the kidnapper.

"It is you who are the fool, Gómez," said Santora. "It is you who led us to the mirror. That is where the secret is hidden, isn't it? All these years. That is the secret of Manolos' power—the Chiavo glass. It will be destroyed!"

"It is mine," insisted Gómez. "It was promised to me. All those years, I worked for him, and he promised the glass would be mine. Only, when he died, that fool of a woman, she sent it out of the country and I was not there because . . ."

"Because you were in jail," said Santora. He seated himself on a packing case. "Poor Juan Gómez. You were in jail when your master died because you tried to pick the pocket of an English tourist. Poor Gómez. You lose. You always lose. The mirror will be destroyed for the good of the republic."

"No!" shouted Gómez. "It is mine! It was promised."

"Manolos lied," Santora announced. "He lied to you. Why did you think he would not lie to you when he lied to everyone else? Did you think you were different? But there is an end to it now. I will destroy the glass."

"You will not!" cried Gómez. "You soft one. I know you. You do not frighten me! You with your smooth face and your smooth manners! You do not frighten me! You will not shed blood!"

The frantic Gómez suddenly hurled himself at the man with the gun.

There was an explosion. A bullet ricocheted off a steel beam and thudded into wood somewhere high above. Santora shouted and tried to fling the smaller man away as one might fling away a nasty animal. The gun flew out of his grip and scudded across the floor.

Santora and Gómez spun around, both intent on the gun. Gómez gave a cry of rage as it skittered through an open trap door and dropped out of sight. There was a splash, and the gun was gone.

Santora pulled himself erect. "So," he said. "Perhaps you are right. Perhaps I would prefer not to shoot you. But you will not leave here with the glass." He picked up a piece of lumber that lay nearby and faced the mirror. "I will do what I came to do," he said. "I will smash this."

Jupiter Jones stepped through the doors from the office into the warehouse. "Before you do that," he said quietly, "there are some questions I'd like to ask."

The man named Juan Gómez gawked at the boys. His eyes lighted on Jeff Parkinson, so recently his hostage. He let out a shout—and charged toward The Investigators.

"Hold it!" shouted Pete. He dodged past Jupiter and hurled himself at the kidnapper's midsection. Gómez went down on the floor, howling, and Pete quickly sat on him. "This is getting to be a habit," said Pete.

"Let me help," offered Jeff, and he sat on Gómez too.

"Now," said Jupiter Jones to the astonished Santora, "we may not be adults, but we are two to one, and nobody leaves here until we find out a few things."

17

The Mirror
Yields Its Secret

Juan Gómez stopped struggling and began muttering under his breath. He sounded as if he might be cursing. "Don't smash the mirror, Señor Santora," said Jeff. "Whether it belongs to you or not, don't smash the mirror. My grandmother would have a fit!"

"Also," said Jupiter Jones, "if you do smash it, you might reveal the secret to Juan Gómez, mightn't you? And I believe he doesn't know what the secret is."

"I know," said Gómez. "Always I have known. But it is the proof I must have."

"Well then," said Jupiter, "I can put it another way. Gómez does not know where in the mirror the proof is hidden. I don't think that you know either, Señor Santora. As for your tale of being a descendant of Chiavo the magician, I think we can dismiss that as pure fiction."

"I will say nothing," said Santora.

"At this point, you need to say very little," Jupiter told him. "We know, for example, that you are acting on the orders of the president of the Republic of Ruffino. Far from being a descendant of Chiavo's, you could very well be, what? Are you President García's son?"

Santora sat down on the packing case. "You!" he said. "It was you who broke into my hotel room. You went through my papers!"

"No, it wasn't Jupe," said Pete. "It was Gómez. He knocked you on the head. I was right outside and I heard the whole thing and saw Gómez leave."

The little man writhed and cursed again. "That one there!" he moaned. "That fine gentleman in his fine clothes! He speaks of the good of the republic! He is the nephew of García, that proud one, that honest man who thinks he is saving Ruffino! A thief! The uncle is a thief and the nephew too."

Jupe cleared his throat. "When President García was elected twelve years ago, his opponent accused him of dishonesty. He said he had proof that García started his career as a criminal. But that opponent couldn't produce the proof, and García won the election. The proof! García must try for reelection this year, mustn't he? Suppose someone could come up with the proof of those charges? What would happen?"

"It would be a tragedy for Ruffino," said Santora.

"The police will be here any minute, Señor Santora," said Jupiter. "We have sent for them. They will want to know why the mirror is so important that Mrs. Darnley's grandson was kidnapped so Gómez could get it. I think I know why."

Santora started up. "You know? But you cannot know!"

"It is a question of blackmail, isn't it, Señor Santora?" said Jupiter Jones. "Isabella Manolos was innocent. She did not know how her husband attained his high position in the government of Ruffino. She didn't know, but we can guess. He had the proof—the proof that the charges against the president were true. He was blackmailing the president."

Santora slumped. "Your police must not find it!" he said. "Before my uncle took office, the people of Ruffino suffered much. There would have been a revolution. Under my uncle there has been peace and good times. There has been progress where before our poor people lived like serfs. We must go on with García. We cannot go back to the bad old ways. There has not been a single blot on my uncle's record. He has surrounded himself with men of wisdom, of honor—except for Manolos, that villain."

"A blackmailer?" Jupe persisted.

Santora nodded sadly. "Very well. I will tell you, and if you know where the mirror's secret is, I think you will tell me."

Santora looked toward Juan Gómez. "That pig on the floor, he was the servant of Diego Manolos. You know what he is—a pickpocket, a sneak thief. Now you tell me he is a kidnapper too. I am not surprised. He is dangerous, without pity and without heart. For ten years he served Manolos, so you can guess what Manolos was. Señora Manolos, the friend of Señora Darnley, she is a lovely lady, but women are sometimes foolish when they choose a husband. She has suffered much for her foolishness."

"Stupid woman!" exclaimed Juan Gómez.

"Silence!" cried Santora. "In his youth my uncle was foolish too, for a time. Many young men are foolish. He was sent to Spain, to the university. There he met Diego Manolos who also was sent to Spain. Manolos had the glass of the magician Chiavo. He had purchased it quite honestly, and perhaps that is the last honest thing he ever did. Chiavo did indeed have a son, and that son had a son and so on, until the last one. The last descendant of the magician was not a son. There was a daughter. She did not marry, and when Manolos found her she was an old woman, very poor, living in a little town in Castile. She had the goblin glass. She had the glass but no money, and money she needed.

"Manolos was poor himself, but young, and he had some imagination, that one. He borrowed the money to buy the glass and he had the glass shipped back to Madrid. He talked of it everywhere—in the cafes and the lecture halls. He had the mirror of Chiavo. The story got round, and there was some wonderment. Could the glass really show the future? Manolos pretended that the power of the mirror was real. He pretended that he could see the future in the glass.

"It did not take long. First some students came to him from the university, and he told them things that would happen. He said things that were not very precise, but the foolish young men wanted to believe. Sometimes what he said happened—or something close enough to it so that they began to think that he did see things in the mirror. Then came the wealthy people from the city, and he told them things too.

"Then Manolos showed his evil. He told one very old man who suffered from the gout that he should take a voyage. The old man went, and while he was away his house was robbed. Manolos told a woman that the money she had should be blessed, that she should take it to her own priest at the church where she always prayed. She did, but on the way to the church her pocket was picked. There were other things. I need not go on. You understand since you seem to have intelligence for ones so young."

"What a confidence operation!" cried Pete. "But didn't the Spanish police catch on?"

"In time," said Santora. "But already, before he started this villainy, Manolos paid special attention to my uncle. Even as a young man my uncle was interested in reform for Ruffino. He talked much of it, and Manolos listened. Manolos thought my uncle would become important and that he should have some influence with my uncle. Also, the Garcías had much money, so Manolos thought of the blackmail. He would use the glass, and he would . . . how do you say it in the movies about gangsters?"

"He would frame your uncle?" suggested Bob.

"*Sí*. Yes. That is it. So Manolos, he had influence on a young girl, a servant in one of the great houses. With his mirror he convinced her that she was being cheated by her employers. He convinced her that she was the victim of an injustice, and that she had the right to avenge herself. He said he knew of a man who would pay a great price for the jewels which belonged to this girl's employer. He said the girl must take the jewels and put them in a box and wrap the box with red paper, and that he would make the arrangements. The man would meet the girl and give her the money in an envelope, and she would give him the jewels. And so she did it. She stole the jewels and met the man whom Manolos described. He gave her an envelope, and she gave him the box wrapped in red paper. And that man was my uncle!"

"A thief!" snarled Juan Gómez.

"My uncle did not know!" cried Santora. "He thought he was only doing a favor for Manolos. He thought he was delivering a letter to the girl, and that she was giving him a gift for Manolos. He met the girl on a street near a fountain. Manolos was there with a camera. Manolos took a photograph of my uncle and the girl, and in the photograph my uncle hands the girl an envelope!"

"Naturally the authorities discovered what had happened," said Jupe.

"But of course they did. The girl opened the envelope and there was no money, only paper. She was very frightened. When her mistress found that the jewels were gone the police came and the girl cried and told everything. Only by that time my uncle was on his way back to Ruffino. He never learned of it. Not for a long time. Manolos got away from Madrid with his mirror and his photograph—and the jewels— just in time. There were stories in the newspapers about him and the evil he had done with that glass."

"So he went to Ruffino and started to blackmail your uncle?" said Pete.

"He went to Ruffino, but he did nothing at first," Santora told him. "He had money, you see, from his crimes. He waited. He married that poor lady, Isabella, because she was the only child of a wealthy man. And he waited. Then, twelve years ago, when it was the time for the election, and we were almost in a revolution—then he acted. He sent my uncle a print of that photograph and copies of those old stories from the Spanish newspapers. My uncle had been involved in a crime and here was the proof. Never mind that García had not known. Never mind that it was so long ago. Here was the proof, and it would ruin my uncle. Never would he win the election.

"So my uncle gave in to that wretch. He gave him money at first, but soon that was not enough. He gave him power. So Manolos had his big house, and some respect—not much. Every year, on the anniversary of the election, my uncle received another print of that photograph and more copies of those old newspaper stories. At last Manolos died, and we hoped—my uncle and I—that the long nightmare was over and the blackmail would stop.

"I went to see Señora Manolos. Poor lady. She was in tears. I wanted to ask her—and it is difficult to do such a thing, because she is truly a lady—if I could search her house. Before I could think how best to say this to her, she complained to me of Juan Gómez. She said she had shipped the mirror to her friend in Los Angeles, and that Gómez, when he discovered this, was very angry. He shouted at her. He called her a fool. She said she feared he was going to strike her.

"So then I knew. The negative of that picture must be hidden in the mirror. The only creature to whom Manolos might have told the secret was Gómez— Gómez, the servant of the pig! And when Gómez left Ruffino that afternoon and took a plane to Los Angeles, I was sure!"

"So you followed, and you tried to buy the mirror from Mrs. Darnley," said Jupiter Jones. "When that didn't work, you told that tale about being a descendant of Chiavo. And when that didn't work, and your uncle urged you to act quickly, you hired the magician Baldini to impersonate the ghost in the glass."

Santora hung his head. "I am ashamed," he said. "I did not wish to frighten women and children, but I could think of no other way."

The boys and Santora paused. From outside the warehouse, there came the sound of heavy footsteps. A door opened.

"Here come the police," said Pete.

He relaxed, starting to get up off Gómez.

"What will we say to the police?" said Santora, very pale. "They will want to examine the mirror!"

"Ha!" Gómez laughed. He twisted away from Pete and Jeff and scrambled to his feet. Grasping the piece of timber which Santora had dropped, he lunged at the mirror. "I will have my proof!" he screamed, "and then no one will dare . . . ."

Suddenly he froze in a half crouch and stared into the dimly lit goblin glass, where his own face was reflected, distorted with rage and fear. He dropped the timber, screamed horribly, and ran. Then he stumbled, his foot twisting under him, and pitched forward through the open trap door.

There was a splash from below, and then there were lights and voices and uniformed men.

Again, from the water beneath the warehouse, came that terrible screaming.

"The negative!" said Santora in a hoarse whisper. "Where is the negative?"

Jupe stepped behind the glass and, with thumb and forefinger, peeled a label off the backing. He handed the label, and something else, to Señor Santora. "Microfilm," he said quietly. "Of course. It couldn't be anything else. Microfilm under one of the labels on the back of the mirror. Under the newest label."

Señor Santora gasped a quick thanks and stuffed the tiny bit of film and the torn label into his coat pocket.

"Jeff Parkinson?" asked a police sergeant. "One of you kids Jeff Parkinson?"

"I am," said Jeff.

Near the trap door two policemen uncoiled a rope. In a moment they had hauled the struggling Gómez out of the water. The kidnapper collapsed on the floor of the warehouse and sobbed.

The police sergeant scowled at the cringing, dripping man, then turned back to Jeff. "Is that your kidnapper?" he asked.

"Yes. His name is Juan Gómez."

"And this man?" The sergeant nodded toward Santora.

"This is Señor Santora," said Jupe simply. "He's a friend. He's been helping us."

"What's the matter with this guy?" called one of the officers who was bending over Gómez.

"The thing!" gasped Gómez. "In the mirror, I saw it! That . . . that . . ."

"What about the mirror?" The sergeant looked curiously at the goblin glass.

"It once belonged to a famous sorcerer," said Jupiter Jones. "It's supposed to be haunted. The kidnapper seems very much afraid of it, doesn't he? Perhaps he thought he saw a ghost."

The policeman snorted.

"A man's imagination can play strange tricks," said Jupiter, "especially in this dim light."

"Yes, I suppose," said the policeman.

The boys and Señor Santora looked at the mirror.

It stood there in the dusty warehouse and reflected the bare walls and the cobwebs. It was a looking glass, a perfectly ordinary old looking glass which happened to have an extremely ugly frame.

But, in spite of themselves, the boys shivered a bit. When the police sergeant asked them to leave, they did not hesitate. They left.

18
An Invitation
for Mr. Hitchcock

It was two weeks later that The Three Investigators called on Mr. Alfred Hitchcock, the famous motion-picture director. Jupiter Jones had an envelope, which he handed to Mr. Hitchcock without comment.

"Oh?" said Mr. Hitchcock. He opened the envelope and took out a sheet of rich-looking, cream-colored stationery. He glanced at the few lines written on the notepaper, then put it down on his desk. "So Mrs. Jonathan Darnley invites me to a dinner party at which I am to have the honor of meeting Señor Rafael Santora," he said. "I know Mrs. Darnley, and I know also that there must be a reason for her to send you with this invitation."

Bob smiled and handed a file folder to Mr. Hitchcock. "I guess this could be considered classified information," he said. "But we told Señor Santora you'd be interested in this case and that you'd keep the facts secret."

"You assume a great deal," said Mr. Hitchcock, and he opened the file.

The boys waited in silence while Mr. Hitchcock read Bob's typed notes on the Case of the Haunted Mirror. Finally the director turned over the last page of the report and looked up at Jupiter.

"I suppose it was the mention of a photograph that let you guess the mirror's secret—and where it was hidden," he said.

"Yes," answered Jupe. "When Señor Santora told how his uncle was being blackmailed with a photograph, I knew there had to be a negative somewhere. Since we had already taken the mirror apart, the only hiding place left was under the labels—the ones that furniture restorers had put on when they repaired the glass. Manolos had put his 'evidence'—the photograph and the old newspaper stories—on microfilm because regular film negatives were too large to hide under a label. Every year Manolos would simply remove the label over the microfilm, make new prints for President García—we have since learned Manolos had a darkroom in his house—and then put the microfilm back under a new label. I suppose he had stolen a supply of fresh labels, or else had had them printed up."

"I am surprised that he trusted Juan Gómez so much," said Mr. Hitchcock. "The man is obviously a thoroughgoing scoundrel. Why would Manolos ever let Gómez know the proof was concealed in the mirror?"

"We'll never know for sure," said Jupiter. "Gómez isn't talking. Perhaps Manolos kept Gómez in line by promising that one day he would have the secret. Perhaps Gómez merely guessed over the years that the mirror was the source of Manolos' power. Gómez probably helped him take it down every year, though I'm sure he wasn't allowed to see what happened next."

"Seems a great deal of trouble to go to over a bit of microfilm," said the director. "He could have hidden it anywhere."

"Manolos *did* have imagination," said Jupiter Jones. "There's a kind of evil poetry in what he did. He used the mirror originally to get that poor servant girl in Madrid to commit a crime. He took advantage of that crime to implicate García, and he hid the incriminating evidence against García right on the mirror."

"One can appreciate the artistry," said Mr. Hitchcock. "And what do the police think of the entire matter?"

"They think Gómez is some kind of a nut," said Pete, "and believe me, nobody's going to tell them different."

Mr. Hitchcock nodded. "And I am sure they will see to it that Gómez will not be at liberty for quite some time. Tell me, how was Gómez able to find Santora's hotel? And how did it happen that Santora showed up at that warehouse in San Pedro at exactly the right moment?"

"Señor Santora and Gómez were both keeping track of each other," answered Jupe. "Each was afraid the other would get the mirror first. We assume that Gómez discovered Santora was in town because he had the Darnley house under surveillance. He probably saw Santora come calling on Mrs. Darnley and trailed him back to his hotel. He knew Santora would get in his way so he attacked him.

"Santora discovered where Gómez was staying by doing what we didn't have time to do. He rented a car and cruised the Silverlake area until he learned where Gómez' cousin lived. By trailing Gómez from there, he learned about the empty farmhouse in the San Fernando valley, though he didn't know why Gómez was interested in it. The day he was released from the hospital, he finally located Gómez at the farmhouse, but he didn't know Jeff was inside. He simply spotted Gómez' car out front and followed it into San Pedro."

"Señor Santora was lucky," said Mr. Hitchcock. "Gómez might have killed him. But what about the magician, Baldini? I believe I've heard the name before."

Jupiter Jones chuckled. "Santora knew about Baldini. He had seen him perform in Ruffino. Baldini was an escape artist, among other things. Santora said that he once saw Baldini handcuffed and wrapped in chains that were fastened with padlocks, and in three seconds he'd picked the locks and was free. Santora was sure Baldini could get into a house that was as securely locked as the Darnley place.

"Santora found Baldini very simply. He called agents who booked night-club acts until he found Baldini's. At first he thought Baldini would have to slip in and out of the house to impersonate the phantom of the glass. But Baldini had known Drakestar, and he knew about that secret door and the hidden room under the library. He just moved in and stayed. Santora was paying him plenty, and Santora convinced him that he only wanted to play a practical joke on Mrs. Darnley.

"Poor Baldini. When we found the hidden door and came down those stairs, he began to think practical jokes weren't funny at all. After he escaped from the Darnley house, he decided he was mixed up in something that was too big for him to handle. He moved out of his rooming house and went into hiding. He didn't want to see us or Santora again.

"Mrs. Darnley has forgiven him, however. She put an ad in *Variety* and also in the *Hollywood Reporter* to let him know everything was all right. He's going to be at the dinner party, by the way. He'll wear Drakestar's robe and do Drakestar's famous disappearing act—using the secret door."

"And that must be an extremely well-built secret door," said Mr. Hitchcock. "I would rather enjoy seeing it."

"You'll see it if you accept the invitation," promised Pete.

"Most intriguing," said Alfred Hitchcock. "And I trust that Henry Anderson, that admirable young bread man, did not get into trouble with his employer?"

"Nope. Seems that all those police around the San Pedro warehouse got hungry and bought up all of Henry's baked goods. His boss was pleased when he returned with an empty truck." Pete grinned and went on. "Now Henry's decided the bakery business is too quiet. He wants to be a private detective! Mrs. Darnley's promised to help him any way she can."

"Excellent," said Mr. Hitchcock. "And you are right, I will keep the facts you have given me in strictest confidence. If you plan to publish this case, I am sure you will do the same. For the good of the republic, change all the names."

"Of course," said Jupiter Jones.

"If I attend the dinner, will I also see the haunted looking glass?" asked Mr. Hitchcock.

Jupe nodded. "But it won't be hanging in the library," he told the director. "Señora Manolos is coming from Ruffino, you see, and she hates that mirror, so Mrs. Darnley has had it moved to the hidden room. I think that Mrs. Darnley doesn't like the glass, either. She almost lost Jeff because of it. Also . . ."

Jupiter Jones stopped and gazed into space.

"Don't tell me she's afraid of it?" said Mr. Hitchcock.

"No. Not really. But Gómez said he saw something in it and . . . well, that was a disaster for Gómez, wasn't it? He is now in jail, and he'll be there for quite a while."

"What do you think?" asked Mr. Hitchcock.

Jupe smiled. "I think it's very ugly, and if I had it, I'd hide it in the basement too."